TROUBLE
On
EUPHORIA LANE

Book Three in
The Homeowners' Association
Cozy Mystery Series

Tina Swayzee McCright

COPYRIGHT

DEDICATION

This book is dedicated to my granddaughter. She fills my heart with love, reminds me to play, and brings a smile to my face every day.

ACKNOWLEDGMENTS

I would like to thank June Brewer, one of my newsletter subscribers, for suggesting the name of one of my characters. Congratulations to Alicia Kozak. She won my newsletter subscriber contest, which awarded her a guest appearance in this book. Also, a special thank you to my launch team, Jeanette, Sue, Mari, my husband Pat, Jackie, and especially Kathryne. I appreciate you more than I can say.

ONE

Andi Stevenson watched her friend Meg toss salt over her shoulder. "Since when did you become superstitious?"

"Since our homeowners' association troubles began attracting the Grim Reaper," Meg said. The high-strung nurse blew salt off her palm and over Andi's shoulder. "I told my aunt we were holding a baking lesson here tonight, and she reminded me that people had either been killed or attacked when we held events in the clubhouse before."

There had only been a handful of occasions where they used the clubhouse over the past couple of years that they had known each other. It seemed like a million years ago since the two of them had met when Andi first moved into the complex. She had just closed on her new condo, a home she had saved for years to buy, and when she tossed out a bag of trash, she found the president of the homeowners' association dead in the dumpster. The vice president took the vacant position, and one thing led to another, which resulted in a neighborhood war. Meg became her closest ally during every battle those first few weeks.

Andi gave Meg a warm smile. "No one has died *inside* the clubhouse," she said. "Plus, I was the only person attacked on the premises, and it was more like a warning than an intent to do bodily harm. Although my neck was sore for a while." She suddenly remembered the point of the conversation was to keep Meg from worrying. "Besides, nothing bad is going to happen tonight," she hastily added, hoping her words proved to be true. "This isn't Cabot Cove in an episode of Murder She Wrote. Half the town isn't going to get whacked one after another until the series concludes."

Meg grimaced. "I hope you're right. Although you do track down the killer just like Jessica Fletcher did in that show."

"The difference is I know self-defense techniques, thanks to my sister's police training." Andi couldn't blame her friend for being concerned. Euphoria Lane Condominiums, located in Glendale, a suburb of Phoenix, Arizona, had more than its share of deaths over the past two years. At least the bad guys were now all behind bars. That should have given Meg some peace of mind, but it obviously didn't.

Both women unpacked a box of baking utensils, arranging each item on the granite countertop. Meg's short, curly-blonde hair bounced with each move. Her overabundance of energy usually brought the clubhouse to life—when she was in a cheerful mood. The small building near the community pool contained an open kitchen at one end and a drab, cream-colored living room at the other.

Suddenly, another smile tugged at Andi's lips. "Roxie's coming tonight. Although I'm positive no one is going to meet their maker, I can't promise there won't be a little mayhem if she drinks more rum than she pours into her rum balls. You know how she can get."

Meg lifted a brow. "I hope she doesn't dance on the furniture."

"Or get sick," Andi said. "I don't want to drag her bony body home *again.*"

The French doors to the clubhouse swung open, and Roxie, an eccentric, retired hairdresser, made her grand entrance. She wore her favorite leopard-print jumpsuit and a dozen gold bracelets. She patted her pink, beehive hairdo with her frighteningly long, acrylic nails painted a bright yellow. "I'm here. Let the fun begin!"

"Fun within reason," Andi warned.

"Where's your box?" Meg leaned to the side as if expecting to see it outside the door. "I thought you were going to bake with us tonight."

"I am." Roxie sashayed across the tile in her cherry-red stilettos, and the aroma of stale cigarettes followed. "I found a young hunk to carry it in for me."

A young hunk? Andi glanced at the open door but could only see trees and their shadows cast by the setting sun. *Maybe Roxie ran into Meg's son.* The college student still lived at home while he attended classes and worked part-time. *I certainly hope she isn't hitting on Chad. The woman is at least three times his age, maybe four.*

The hunk suddenly stepped into view. He carried in a cardboard box with ROXIE printed in black block letters on the side. His dark hair, turning gray at the temples, and crow's feet fanning out from his eyes surprised Andi. *I didn't realize 'young' meant early fifties—if my guess is correct.*

Andi hadn't seen the man with the dazzling blue eyes before. She turned to find Meg gaping at the newcomer.

"Stop drooling, ladies," Roxie said. "You'll scare off the single man, and we all know how rare those are around here."

Andi felt her face turn red. "I'm taken." She quickly pointed to her friend. "She's not."

"What?!" Meg's eyes widened. She turned to the hunk, "I'm not...not..."

"Able to complete a coherent sentence." Roxie's laugh sounded like a cackle.

Andi wasn't sure what to think of Meg's reaction to the newcomer. She usually wasn't interested in the single men who moved into the neighborhood. She had divorced her husband years ago after he ran off with his secretary, and since then, trust issues had kept her from dating much while raising her son alone.

"You can place the box over here on the kitchen island," Andi said, while narrowing her eyes in warning toward the older woman who sometimes helped out with paperwork at the detective agency Andi's sister bought. "And please don't listen to Roxie. She has a *unique* sense of humor."

Roxie waved her off. "Don't hate me because I'm beautiful," she said, mimicking a line from an old shampoo commercial.

The hunk smiled, and his bright white teeth flashed like a neon sign. "I'm Mack." He gently set the box down on the island. "I didn't mean to disrupt your evening." He glanced over at Meg with a twinkle in his eyes. "Or cause you any embarrassment."

Meg blushed again. The rose tint made the over-forty mother look like a teenager.

Roxie reached inside her bra for a compact mirror and began checking her makeup. "I bumped into Mack on my way over. He's renting the Owens' condo and doesn't even mind that someone bit the big one there. I'm impressed! You couldn't catch me in that place—unless there's a séance." She snapped the compact shut. "Are you planning on having a séance? I have the perfect outfit if you are."

"I haven't given it any thought," Mack said. "To be honest, I rented the place because death has a way of lowering the rent, even in a complex that backs up to a golf course." His pricey black, button-up shirt and dark jeans didn't scream pinching pennies, but then he might shop for clothes when they were on sale. Andi usually did.

"Lucky for you, you're not as frightened of the possibility of ghosts as we are." Andi shuddered at her horrible memories of the place. She'd almost died in that garage. Even her boyfriend Luke avoided walking near the Owens' condo. *So why isn't Mack afraid? Is he used to dead bodies?* "By any chance, are you a doctor?"

"Not the kind that carries a stethoscope," he said, removing an electric mixer from Roxie's box.

"Coroner?" Meg guessed with a grimace.

"Mortician?" Roxie offered her guess in a tone that reflected her hope of winning this new game.

"Retired dentist," he said, placing the mixer on the counter.

"That explains it." Roxie waved off the answer as if every dentist would move into a haunted condo.

Meg and Andi exchanged questioning glances.

"What?" Roxie accepted the spatula he handed her. "He's used to gross stuff. If you can shove your hands into a bleeding mouth and pull out black teeth, you can sleep in a house with ghosts." Not that anyone had seen a ghost in the Owens' condo, just flickering lights accompanied by strange noises.

Mack lifted a brow. "I did wear gloves when I *shoved my hands into bleeding mouths*, but I understand your meaning." He turned to Andi. "I wouldn't mind learning how to bake. Is this class restricted to people who have already registered?"

"No, it's not," Meg said, before turning away to busy herself with the measuring cups.

When she didn't continue, Andi said, "We would be glad to have you join us. It's nothing official, just a few members of the homeowners' association board of directors teaching other neighbors how to bake some of our favorite cookies in preparation for the holidays. Frankly, we could use more participants. The neighbors who wanted us to hold the class after our last bake sale didn't sign up. They have other commitments."

"It's only October," Mack said. "Do people usually do their holiday baking this soon?"

"We're starting with Halloween cookies," Roxie said. "Besides, you can freeze cookies. You can freeze anything—which reminds me of Mrs. Owens."

Andi shook her head, not wanting to scare Mack out of the neighborhood. "Another time." *Hopefully, never.*

"In December, we're going to have a big community cookie exchange," Meg said, continuing their original conversation.

She appeared to have overcome her initial tongue-tied reaction to Mack, which was a relief to Andi. She didn't want to spend the evening trying to yank her friend out of a trance-like state.

"A cookie exchange?" He arched a brow in apparent confusion.

Andi turned her attention back to Mack. "Everyone who wants to participate brings three dozen cookies, and we divide them up." When she noticed he looked more confused, she said, "We'll go into more detail later. In the meantime, let's find you a partner."

Roxie pointed at Meg with one of her lethal fingernails, while a twinkle lit her hazel-colored eyes. "Mack can help *her*. She needs someone who knows what to do with his hands."

Meg narrowed her eyes into slits. "Roxie!"

The older woman shrugged in response. "He's a dentist. He's used to working in tiny places. He can help you draw the legs where you want them, so you don't have a mess on your hands."

Andi stifled a groan and quickly explained. "Meg's cookies are spiders with melted chocolate legs."

"You need to get your mind out of the gutter." Roxie smirked while she shoved her compact mirror back into her bra, which reminded Andi of a magical, bottomless bag. She hated to think what all Roxie kept hidden in there—besides a mirror and cigarette butts.

The doors opened to the sound of women's voices. Betsy, one of Roxie's friends and a fellow member of a water aerobics group called The Water Guppies, brought a warm smile and pleasant attitude into the room. "Look who I found waiting outside."

Andi instantly recognized another new neighbor. She would be hard to miss with her long, red hair. Andi's red highlights streaking her brunette hair were nothing compared to this woman. She would stand out in a crowded convention center. "Poppy, I'm so glad you decided to join us!"

The attractive, thin woman, who appeared to be close to thirty, hesitated before stepping inside.

"Come on," Betsy urged. "No one here bites, except for maybe Roxie."

Meg and Andi both chuckled but then quickly snapped their mouths shut.

Roxie merely shrugged. "It depends on who I'm looking at. You're safe, girly. I rarely bite women and never ones without meat on their bones. It might break my dentures."

Poppy's green eyes widened in fear.

"Don't listen to her," Andi said. She considered making that the theme for the evening. "Poppy, you'll be baking with me tonight. Betsy, you're with Roxie."

"Yum! Rum balls!" Betsy almost danced her way over to the kitchen island. She made quick work of putting on the apron she'd brought with her to protect one of her many new, dressy pantsuits. After tying the white apron behind her back, she pushed shoulder-length strands of her sleek, gray hair behind her ear.

Andi wasn't the only one who had noticed that Betsy had recently gone through an expensive makeover, car included. She used to wear baggy, pastel jogging suits every day. One rumor was that she had inherited a ton of money. Roxie liked to tell everyone who would listen that Betsy had robbed a bank in Louisiana and was a fugitive from the law. Thankfully, no one paid much attention to her stories. Betsy was a sweet woman and a great neighbor. You could always count on her to help where needed around the complex.

Poppy helped Andi line up the dry ingredients on the counter. The two of them had met for the first time at the mailboxes the previous day. Poppy mentioned she had recently moved to Arizona from Chicago and didn't know anyone in the complex yet, and Andi thought it would do her good to attend the class to meet some of the neighbors.

"All right, everyone," Andi said. "Let's go ahead and get started. We'll be preparing our favorite cookies during three evening sessions. We'll rotate partners each time we get together, so you'll get a chance to learn baking tips from each instructor."

"Do we get a doggy bag to take home?" Betsy's voice sounded hopeful.

Meg nodded enthusiastically. "We're going to divide the cookies between us."

Andi was looking forward to sampling their creations as much as the others. "Roxie is making rum balls with zombie faces painted on with fondant icing."

At the mention of her name, Roxie removed a shot glass from her bra and proceeded to fill it to the rim with the amber liquid. Mack blinked rapidly.

7

Andi continued before anyone asked Roxie how she managed to hide a shot glass beneath her clothing without the outline showing. "Meg, please tell Poppy and Betsy what you're baking tonight."

"Peanut butter spider cookies. I was going to run by the dollar store to buy tins to put them in, but I ended up working extra hours at the hospital."

"Meg is a nurse," Andi told the newcomers. "She works in the emergency room."

Mack nodded his approval, and Andi could swear he gazed upon Meg with new appreciation.

"I'm baking bull's eye cookies," Andi said. "We can use frosting to draw a ghastly character like a ghost or witch in the center of each target."

"Or an ex-husband," Poppy said. Her statement drew the attention of everyone in the room. "I just got a divorce," she explained quietly.

"I can relate." Meg sighed. "Although mine was a long time ago. I found it helpful to focus on anything besides *him*."

Poppy offered a warm smile in response. "I decided to change everything about my life, starting with attending the veterinarian school a couple of miles away. I've always loved animals."

"Here's to animals!" Roxie held up her shot glass. "And to divorce." She threw back the liquid and swallowed loudly. "Enough blabbing, I'm ready to rumball! Get it? Rum ball, rumble?"

Betsy gave her a thumbs-up gesture. "That's a good one."

The three teams set to work, although Meg looked uncomfortable with Mack watching her every move. Andi had never seen her this way before. She couldn't wait to get her alone later to talk.

After measuring the flour, Andi turned to her baking partner. "Are you settling into your condo?"

Poppy nodded. "I almost have everything unpacked, and the cable was already working the day I moved in. The owner is so nice! When he found out I was a student at the veterinary school, he offered to give me a lease based on the rest of the school year and not a calendar year, just in case I decide to move back home."

"That *was* nice." Andi reached for the bag of confectioners' sugar. "Where were you staying before here?" She didn't know a lot about the school, but she did know classes started in August or September, not October.

"I shared an apartment with another student when I first moved to Arizona, but the neighbors were too loud. I heard about this complex from one of my instructors. He said it was quiet because most of the neighbors are..."

Andi smiled. "Old?"

Poppy bit her lip.

"It's okay," Andi said. "Yes, at least half of our neighbors are over the age of sixty, but many are around thirty to forty, so not everyone is ancient." She caught Roxie's glare and chuckled. "The college students who like to party tend to hang out at the pool on the weekends. Luckily, your condo is far from that area. Their noise won't disturb your studies."

"That's a relief. I'm going to need quiet to keep up with these classes."

Soon, a gentle hum filled the room as everyone worked. Andi watched Poppy flatten the cream-colored dough on parchment paper. Andi had just finished flattening the cocoa-colored dough. They layered and rolled the dough into cylinders. Their cookies would look similar to archery targets with dark and light circles once they were baked.

"I can't wait to see how this recipe turns out," Andi said. "I included a few tips I learned from Martha Stewart."

"You know Martha Stewart?!"

Andi grinned. "I'm afraid not. I read her recipe books and check out her website for helpful hints, but I don't stop there. I experiment with recipes I find in books and online, add a twist here or there, and eventually come up with a version I prefer." She collected the rolled-up dough. "I'm going to place these in the refrigerator for twenty minutes," Andi said. "Do you want some coffee while we wait? I can make a fresh pot."

"I would love some." Poppy reached for a wet cloth.

"While you're busy, I'll clean up the flour."

Andi glanced in her friend's direction as she headed to the refrigerator. Meg was telling Mack all about The Water Guppies and the way they had turned exercise into a drinking game. He looked amused and asked questions while he stirred their ingredients in a large bowl. Andi felt better, knowing her friend was acting more like herself.

"Oh, no!" Poppy took several steps back, away from the counter. "You have ants!"

"Really?" Andi groaned, then placed the dough in the refrigerator and returned to their station. They shouldn't have any bugs, the homeowners' association, which she currently presided over as president, paid a monthly fee to keep all creepy crawlies far away.

Sure enough, she found a trail of ants traveling along the grout line between the tile and the cupboards. "I can't believe this! Our guy just sprayed in here yesterday."

"I hate to point this out," Poppy said, "but your guy isn't doing his job correctly if you already have ants again. My cousin is an exterminator—a good one. He'll come out for one free treatment as a favor to me." When Andi started to speak, Poppy lifted her hand. "Let me do this for you. It's my way of thanking you for adding me to the class and showing me your techniques. I heard about a girl who paid for college by selling homemade pies. Who knows, maybe I can pay off my tuition selling homemade cookies, and it would all be due to you and this class."

She has a point. Our guy isn't doing his job correctly if we have ants. "I'll take you up on your offer, Poppy. And if your cousin is as good as you say he is, I'll recommend to the rest of the board that we switch our account."

"I'll call him first thing in the morning." Poppy grabbed the broom from the corner. She swept the ants into the dustpan and quickly carried them outside. When she returned, she rushed over to Andi. "There's a woman on her way in, and she is raging mad."

"What does she look—" Before Andi could finish her question, Gladys, one of the older women in the complex who was *not* a Water Guppy, marched inside.

"Betsy, I need to talk to you!" Gladys made a beeline

toward Roxie's baking partner.

Betsy lifted her hands in a halt position. "Gladys, we are in the middle of a baking lesson here. Come over to my place tomorrow, and we'll have tea."

Gladys's bloodshot eyes showed signs of crying from beneath her oversized, blue-framed glasses. "I need to know how you're making your money, and I need to know now! My daughter says she is going to move me back home to Ohio if I can't pay off my credit card bill this month! I didn't mean to charge so much. You have to help me!"

That question silenced the entire room. Everyone wanted to know how Betsy had amassed her sudden wealth.

Betsy's gaze traveled the room. "I'm...a secret shopper."

Meg shoved her baking sheet into the hot oven and then closed the door with a bang. "Even I know secret shoppers don't make that much money."

"I need to know the truth!" Betsy snatched the rolling pin off the counter and threw it across the clubhouse. Her furious expression was more dramatic than the rolling pin landing on the thick, beige carpet with a slight thud. "It's not fair that you're making all of this money and not telling us how!"

Betsy glanced down at her shiny new leather pumps. "I didn't want you to lose your money and blame me."

"She's been gambling at the casinos," Roxie said matter-of-factly as she filled her shot glass again. "I've been telling her to stop before her luck runs out, but she won't listen. It's an addiction." Roxie offered the rest of the bottle to Gladys. "You're going to need this if you're going to spend your winters in Ohio."

"You witch!" Gladys glared at Roxie while she stepped backward until she bumped into the sink. "You and your Water Guppies are a bunch of evil witches!"

"No," Roxie said. "Only me." Her voice didn't sound as sarcastic as usual. Andi thought she detected a hint of sympathy.

Tears streamed down Gladys's face. "You'll get yours," she said with an evil glare. "I just wish I could be around to see how you fall."

Betsy glanced over at Roxie, who gave a slight shake of her head—a secret conversation between the two of them that Andi caught, but no one else seemed to notice.

Gladys ran out of the room. In her haste, she bumped into a mirror clock hanging on the wall. It fell to the tile floor and shattered.

"I guess her next seven years in Ohio aren't going to be good ones." Roxie swallowed a gulp of rum and then wiped away a drop of liquid left on the corner of her mouth with the side of her hand.

"Oh, shut up!" Betsy headed toward the door, but Roxie grabbed her arm.

"You should stay here," the older woman said. "You can't help her."

Betsy's gaze traveled back to the door. "She shouldn't have to leave her home because of credit card debt. Not when..."

Andi didn't know what to say to their new neighbors. Both Mack and Poppy watched with wide-eyed wonder.

"How much have you made gambling?" Mack asked.

"Enough. I've made more than enough." Betsy yanked her arm away from Roxie and then hastily untied her apron. She tossed it on the counter and marched out the door.

Roxie shook her head and then returned to her liquor bottle.

"We should finish up here," Andi said.

"I should call it a night." Poppy edged away from the counter. "Thank you for inviting me."

"I'm sorry about all of this. I'll bring you a plate of cookies tomorrow." Andi wanted to say that life on Euphoria Lane wasn't usually so dramatic, but that would have been a lie. Meg was right, trouble had come to their complex, and it was here to stay.

After Poppy left, the rest of the group spent the next hour finishing their confectionary treats. Roxie drew zombie faces on her rum balls, while Andi used stencils to create ghosts and witch hats inside the targets of her bull's eye cookies. Meg showed Mack how to create spiders on top of their cookies using miniature peanut butter cups, melted chocolate chips, and candy eyes. Words were rarely spoken and only if necessary. Not what Andi had planned.

Mack helped Meg clean up their area and then excused himself with his plate of cookies in hand. She looked like a lost puppy when he left without asking for her phone number.

"You two sure know how to zap the fun out of an evening," Roxie said.

Meg planted her hands on her hips. "How is this our fault?"

"Not enough rum." Roxie tossed her empty bottle into the plastic trash can. "I'm going to take Betsy her plate of cookies. I'll pick up my box tomorrow, or better yet, leave it in the pantry." On her way out, she tossed back over her shoulder, "Next time, lock the door after we're all inside. We don't need any more uninvited guests."

That isn't a bad idea.

Meg grabbed the broom. "I'll sweep up while you finish wiping down the counters."

Andi waited for Roxie to shut the door behind her before speaking her mind. "Do you think Betsy plans to help Gladys with her credit card debt? Betsy looked guilt-ridden when she left."

Meg shrugged. "I was wondering that myself. It might depend on how much Gladys owes." She swept flour into a small pile. "Do you think Betsy is counting cards at the casino?"

"I don't think she knows what it means to count cards. I know I don't."

"I believe it has to do with the probability of a high-scoring card ending up in your hand based on what has already been played." Meg swept the flour into a dustpan and then tossed it into the trash can. "But I wouldn't know what to do with that information, and I don't know how that can help you win the kind of money Betsy has been flaunting. That new car of hers had to cost as much as I make in a year."

"Betsy has trouble remembering what day it is," Andi said. "I don't see her doing anything more difficult than betting on the lottery and asking the clerk if she won."

At ten o'clock, they locked up the clubhouse, along with their baking supplies, and carried their plates of goodies toward their condos. The temperature had to be in the high seventies, despite the late hour. Daily temperatures wouldn't dip into the sixties until after Halloween. In the distance, a lightning bolt struck. Andi counted to ten before hearing the thunder rumble. *Ten divided by five.* "The storm is two miles away."

Meg glanced up at the sky. "I should get home before the wind starts blowing dust everywhere."

"I'll call you tomorrow," Andi said. "I want to get your impression of Mack."

Meg blushed. "He does make an impression, that's for sure. Let's meet for coffee. We can talk then."

Andi walked the path to her front door, wishing her sister was back from her romantic getaway with her boyfriend. Thunderstorms made her nervous, especially when the condo felt dark and empty inside. She unlocked her front door, pushed it open, and then pocketed the keys while holding the plate of cookies with one hand. About to enter her home, she spotted another bolt of lightning streak the sky overhead. At the same time a woman's voice, sounding several buildings away, split the warm night air with a blood-curdling scream.

****

Andi rushed to place her plate of cookies inside and then ran in the direction of the screams for help. A warm wind appeared out of nowhere, whipping up dust and leaves from the ground.

Meg sprinted from her condo, meeting Andi in the middle of the road that circled the complex. "Sounds like Roxie."

"I would recognize that hoarse voice anywhere." Andi pumped her arms as they rounded the corner in record time—record time *for them.*

Up ahead, Roxie raced to the sidewalk by taking quick but tiny steps in her stilettos. "Help! She's dead! Help!"

Doors opened, and neighbors stepped outside to see what the commotion was all about. Some retreated indoors to look out their windows when the wind whistled through the trees and tiny drops of rain dotted the sidewalks.

Andi reached Roxie and took in a deep breath after their short run. The air smelled like a mixture of dirt and rain. "Who's..." She glanced guiltily in Meg's direction.

"You said no one was going to die tonight," she said pointedly.

"I said we wouldn't find a dead body—and we didn't." Andi grimaced and pointed at Roxie. "She did."

"Squabble later. It's Betsy!" Roxie turned back toward the open door. "Follow me!"

Andi's heart grew heavy in her chest.

"Are you sure she's dead?" Meg's tone held the smallest hint of hope.

"It doesn't take a medical professional to know what dead looks like." Roxie's heels clacked on the concrete path to the door. "The fact someone left a pillow over her head and a bull's eye cookie on top of her body proves it was murder. I don't need to be Sherlock Holmes to figure that one out either."

Andi followed Meg inside the recently updated condo. The kitchen to their left contained black stainless steel appliances and quartz countertops. A circular glass table in the dining room held two dozen pink roses in a crystal vase. Their fresh aroma filled the air.

"She's in the master bedroom." Roxie waved them toward the small hallway.

Meg pressed her cell phone into Roxie's hand. "Call nine-one-one."

When Andi entered the bedroom, she sucked in her cheeks to keep from gasping. A floral comforter on the queen-sized bed covered Betsy's body up to her neck. She looked like a fragile child who had been tucked into bed by a parent. Like Roxie had said, a bull's eye cookie sat on top of her chest. Someone had printed BETSY with white decorating gel on top of the black witch's hat in the center of the target on the cookie. Her head rested on one pillow while the other pillow had been thrown to the carpet, presumably by Roxie when she discovered the body. She did say someone had placed a pillow over Betsy's head.

Meg lifted the woman's tiny, limp wrist to take her pulse.

Andi could tell she was no longer with the living. The older woman was right about knowing what death looked like.

Tears slid down Meg's cheek. "I'm used to this at work but not in my own neighborhood and not with someone I saw often and liked." She glanced up at Andi. "I don't get it. Why are we suddenly the murder capital of the world?"

Andi shook her head, not knowing what to say. "Maybe it has to do with that Law of Attraction. We keep thinking about murder, so we attract more of it."

"Are you blaming this on me?" Meg look horrified. "This is my fault because I said I didn't want to find another dead body tonight?"

"No! Of course, not." Andi threw her hands up in the air. "I would never accuse you! The fact is, it's hard not to think about dead people if you've lived in this complex the past couple of years. Just last week, my sister and I were talking about the woman who died in the fountain."

Roxie walked in, bringing the aroma of cigarettes with her. She handed Meg her phone and then pointed to the open decorative box on top of the mahogany dresser. "I noticed when I found Betsy that someone had taken her jewelry, but I don't think it was a burglar who killed her."

"You're right. A burglar wouldn't write her name on a cookie and leave it on her body." Andi scanned the room for anything that might point to the identity of the killer.

"You need to investigate," Roxie said. "Betsy was my friend. Someone has to pay for this!"

"The police will handle it," Meg said.

"Not like Andi can." Roxie choked on the emotion caught in her throat and, most likely, the tar and nicotine from the cigarettes she chain-smoked. "They have a ton of cases to solve. Andi doesn't have any right now."

True. Andi's sister Jessie scheduled her vacation after they solved their last case. They had enough money coming in to wait until after she returned in two weeks to take on more clients.

Roxie sat on the bed, not seeming to care that Betsy's feet rested six inches away. "You quit your teaching job to work for Jessie's detective agency because you're good at investigating crimes," she reminded Andi. "You have the time to find this killer, and you know you want to."

"I..." Andi remembered Betsy's bright smile earlier that night. She was always kind to others. The poor woman didn't deserve to die like this. "Okay, I'll investigate." She removed her phone from her back pocket and started snapping pictures of the room.

"What can we do?" Meg rubbed her arms as she looked around. "If you're investigating, we're helping. Betsy was one of our neighborhood grandmas. She was important to all of us."

"Use your phone to take pictures of everything you see in the other rooms," Andi said, "but don't touch anything. And work quickly, the police will kick us out once they get here."

"What about me?" Roxie said. "I didn't bring my phone."

"You can answer my questions—truthfully for a change." Andi stepped into the open closet. The light from the bedroom lamp streamed inside, enabling her to study the small space and take pictures. Betsy had quite the collection of shoes and purses, all neatly displayed on racks and hooks. A burglar would have searched the room unless Roxie's arrival had scared him off. She walked over to the bedroom window and peered between the blinds. It was unlocked and open, just as she suspected it might be.

She glanced at Roxie, who watched her every move. "If you want me to investigate, you need to tell me how Betsy made her money."

"I told you—gambling." Roxie turned away as if unable to maintain eye contact. "She bet on anything with legs or a number."

The woman's inability to tell the truth—at least not the whole truth—irritated Andi to no end, but she let the subject drop for now. "How did you get in? And how did the killer get one of the cookies I baked tonight?"

"I dropped off her plate of cookies, and we talked for a few minutes. I wanted to make sure she was okay after Gladys's temper tantrum." Roxie kept speaking as she followed Andi into the kitchen. "After I got home, I realized I left my plate of cookies here. Rum makes me hungry, so I came back for it—only Betsy didn't answer the bell."

Andi headed to the stainless steel trash can. She stepped on the lever near the floor that flipped the lid open, making it possible to peek inside without leaving any fingerprints behind. "Was the door unlocked?"

"It was open. Not all the way, about three inches. I thought it was strange because I closed it when I left."

"Did you hear her lock it behind you?"

"No." Roxie's despair deepened her worry lines, making her look ten years older. This was one of those rare times that the kooky woman showed emotion for someone else. They must have been closer friends than anyone knew.

A tube of white decorating gel poked out of the trash. Andi made a mental note to tell the police. *I hope they find prints on the tube. If so, and they are in the system, this case could be wrapped up in no time.* But the thought didn't sit right in her gut. *I doubt it will be that simple.* "Roxie, do you know anything about this decorating gel?"

Roxie peered into the trash can. "Betsy kept baking supplies in her pantry." She pointed to the plate of cookies on the kitchen counter. "It's obvious what happened. Someone killed Betsy, then wrote her name on one of your cookies, and placed it on her chest like a calling card or a message."

Andi noticed some of the cookies were missing, but the ones with the ghosts drawn on them remained on the plate. "The killer chose the cookie with a witch's hat on it, maybe that's part of the message."

"Betsy was a witch?" Roxie asked.

"Not literally," Andi said. "Remember when Gladys called all of The Water Guppies witches?"

Roxie frowned. "You think Gladys killed her?"

"I'm not sure what I think." Andi tried to picture what might have happened. "If someone tried to smother me,

I'm pretty sure I would wake up and put up a fight." It was hard to imagine two tiny, older women fighting to the death. *They would have been evenly matched, and there wasn't any sign of a struggle.*

Meg entered the kitchen. "I didn't see anything strange in the guest room, but I did find a bottle of sleeping pills on the bathroom counter."

"Oh, yeah," Roxie said. "Betsy said she'd taken some of those before I came over the first time. She was already dressed in her nightgown and yawning a lot. She probably went straight to bed and passed out."

Andi frowned. "That would have made it a lot easier to suffocate her with a pillow. Our killer could be anyone."

****

Mack heard the sirens over the bombs blasting in the war movie playing on the television he'd bought after he agreed to move to Euphoria Lane temporarily. He planned to hang it in the spare room of his home, only five miles away, once he was done here. The rest of the furniture in the condo had been rented for him by an agency he'd hired. Nothing fancy and definitely nothing he would buy for himself. Everything was brown. Brown sofa, brown blankets, brown tea towels. Boring and brown, but it did look like a bachelor's home.

He used the remote to turn off the television. The sirens grew closer, and soon he could see the red and blue flashing lights glowing through the slits in his blinds. He pulled on his tennis shoes and baseball cap, then slipped out his front door. Two police cruisers lit up the night in front of a building down the street from his. Neighbors lined the road as they gathered to watch and wait for any news of what had happened.

A group of older women huddling together caught his eye. He suspected they might be members of The Water Gruppy group Betsy and Roxie belong to and decided he should get closer.

He crossed the road, careful to avoid the area lit by the nearest streetlamp. A sudden wind carried the dust-filled aroma of rain, but he didn't feel any drops. A streak of lightning lit up the sky in the distance. It wouldn't be the first time a storm traveled around the complex without leaving more than a few drops of rain.

Mack made sure he kept his head down as he followed the path of the sidewalk, until he passed the three women still huddled together. Next, he worked his way behind the crowd. He carefully considered his options. A middle-aged couple stood next to his targets. They all watched the police officers going in and out of the condo across the road, while discussing what they thought might have happened. He stole glances at the three older women as he pretended to join the middle-aged couple. He listened carefully to everyone around him.

The aroma of lavender and cherry throat lozenges overpowered the smell of rain as he stood near the woman who reminded him of Mrs. Santa Claus with her gray hair and round face with large apple cheeks.

"I can't believe someone broke into Betsy's condo!" Mrs. Claus told her friends. "I told you someone broke into my cousin's house two days ago."

"Could both burglaries be connected?" the soft voice came from the petite woman to Mrs. Claus's right. Her long, wavy blonde hair made her look younger than the other women, but not by much. She reminded him of a spunky elf. The Lord of the Rings type of elf, not the Christmas kind.

"I hope not!" came the voice of the third woman. She wore her gray hair in an attractive style that curled under on her shoulders. She looked like a politician. "That would mean..."

"Don't even go there!" Mrs. Claus said. "Here comes Roxie! She can tell us what's going on."

Mack turned his head away, hoping Roxie wouldn't recognize him standing there in the dimly-lit area with the other neighbors. The fact he'd changed into sweatpants and a pullover shirt after the baking lesson improved his chances.

"What happened?" Mrs. Claus asked.

"Someone murdered Betsy!" Roxie whispered in her

hoarse smoker's voice—louder than she probably had intended. "She was smothered with her own pillow."

The other women gasped.

"Gladys threatened her when we were baking cookies in the clubhouse," Roxie said. "She's probably the one who knocked her off."

"Gladys?" Mrs. Claus shook her head. "No, not Gladys."

Mack agreed with her. He had a hard time believing the frail, although angry, woman he'd watched at the baking lesson could kill anything larger than an annoying insect. When she threw the rolling pin, it barely flew ten feet. *Not enough rage or muscle to commit murder.*

"Let's meet at the pool tomorrow," Mrs. Claus said. "You can tell us everything you know then."

"Ten o'clock." Roxie stepped away from the group and walked back across the road toward the police cruisers.

"I think we should stop," the spunky elf told the others.

"We can't!" the politician insisted vehemently in her whisper. "My daughter has to have knee surgery next month, and I promised to pay for it. Her insurance deductible is six thousand dollars! She doesn't have that kind of money."

"Keep your promise," the spunky elf said. "I don't think anyone knows about us, but we should be extra careful just the same. And stay away from Gladys just in case she is the murderer."

"Poor Betsy," Mrs. Claus cried. The others consoled her for a few minutes and then said their goodbyes.

Meanwhile, across the road, Meg and Andi stepped out of Betsy's condo. They stopped beneath the porch light to speak to Roxie.

He couldn't help but notice the way Meg's curly, blonde hair bounced on her shoulders whenever she moved. He suppressed a smile when he realized he always did have a thing for nurses. He found their caring natures appealing, but there was something extra special about Meg that pulled him toward her. Maybe it was the sparkle in her eyes or how vulnerable she seemed when she couldn't look him in the eye. Yet he knew she had to be resilient to raise a son on her own. A few strokes on his laptop had revealed a lot about the neighborhood nurse. A lot that he liked and admired.

Suddenly, Roxie turned to face the crowd of neighbors. He couldn't let her see him standing so close to where she had been talking to her friends. He quickly slipped into the shadows cast by the trees.

There would be plenty of time to admire the cute nurse later—much later.

TWO

The next morning, Andi met Roxie in front of Betsy's condo. They stood in the road that surrounded the complex, facing the yellow crime scene tape draped from tree to tree like party decorations. A feeling of overwhelming sadness hit Andi quite unexpectantly. *Betsy will never celebrate another birthday.* "I can't believe someone would murder a grandma."

"This world is an evil place, I tell you." Roxie turned at the sound of a door closing. A former rancher, known as The Cowboy, picked his newspaper up off the patch of grass in front of his condo and then waved. Roxie discreetly tugged on the zipper of her neon-green jumpsuit with white feathered sleeves, increasing the amount of cleavage she revealed to the world. She posed with her hand on her hip. The seventy-plus, deeply tanned, retiree smiled and waved goodbye as he walked back to his door.

"You should ask him out," Andi said, trying not to show her amusement.

"I don't want to look desperate." Roxie shuffled alongside the yellow tape bordering Betsy's condo. "You need to stop standing there and get to work on this case. No one around here is going to get a good night's sleep until this guy is behind bars."

"Guy or girl," she corrected.

"I highly doubt that." Roxie rolled her eyes. "Women don't kill other elderly women unless they're after an inheritance. The exception being annoying men, especially ex-husbands. Mine's lucky to be alive."

Roxie changed the subject back to the case, but her words barely penetrated Andi's mind as she stared at the woman's mint-green hair. She couldn't imagine that color coming in a box at the store. At least Roxie wasn't wearing stilettos. Today, it was four-inch wedges. "How do you walk in those things?"

"Carefully. Now where to, Sherlock?"

"Since we can't snoop around inside, let's visit Gladys."

Euphoria Lane was a gated community with two hundred condominiums. Unlike some of the newer developments that often chose desert landscape, this older suburb of Phoenix opted for grass, a variety of trees that included pine, and flowering bushes.

The two of them chatted as they walked the short distance. "I don't think Gladys did it," Roxie said.

"Because she's a woman?"

"And because she's a wimp. Sure, she can throw a rolling pin a few feet, but can she hit someone with it?"

Dumbfounded, Andi stopped and studied the other woman, who broke into a fit of laughter.

"You heard I broke someone's kneecaps with a rolling pin." Roxie slapped her leg in a gesture of exaggerated hilarity.

How can she laugh at such a horrible act of violence? "Did you?"

"I started that rumor when some jerk refused to pay Buddy what he owed. When I showed up at his door with a rolling pin, he handed over every penny." Buddy, her son, was the friendly neighborhood bookie. Roxie sometimes acted as his enforcer, but Andi didn't know what that entailed.

"You didn't answer my question."

"I know." Roxie grinned as she walked down Gladys's sidewalk on her towering shoes. Between her skinny legs and feathered sleeves, she looked like a hen with a mint-green comb on her head. She suddenly stepped off the concrete and onto the grass.

A gleam of sunlight reflected off a silver object. "What is it?"

Roxie wobbled as she bent low. "Betsy's butterfly necklace. I remember the diamond chips on the wings. I doubt it's worth much, but it sure is pretty."

When she reached out with her age-spotted hands and frighteningly long fingernails, Andi yelled, "No! Don't touch it! You'll smudge the fingerprints—if there are any."

"We can't leave it here."

"It's evidence," Andi said. "We need to report it. You stay here and guard the necklace while I talk to Gladys. We can call the detective in charge of the case *after* I come back outside."

"What? Me? Wait out here, twiddling my thumbs? I don't think so." Roxie glanced back down at the butterfly. "Come to think of it—this can't be Betsy's necklace. Hers was gold." She snatched the piece of jewelry from the grass and shoved it into her bra. "We'll both talk to Gladys."

Andi blew out an exasperated breath. "I'm reporting it to the detective, whether you like it or not."

"You know where to find it," Roxie said with a satisfied smirk. "Whether *you* like it or not."

Andi clenched her jaw. "I'm smart enough to leave hazardous missions to the police and military."

"They wish." Roxie patted her chest before marching toward the front stoop.

Gladys answered the door on the third knock. She wore a pastel-blue robe and faux fur house slippers. Her nose was red, and her eyes were puffy from crying. "I heard about Betsy."

"Did you kill her?" Roxie glared at the emotional woman. "You said she would get hers, and you wanted to be around to see her fall."

"I didn't want her to die!" Gladys's crying intensified to the point where her chest heaved. "I wanted her...to get a flat tire...or a month of bad-hair days, not..."

"Of course you didn't want her to die," Andi said softly. "Can we come in and talk? We won't take much of your time, I promise."

Without saying a word, Gladys walked over to a box of tissues on her coffee table. She wiped her eyes, blew her nose, and then fell onto a wingback chair. She didn't say they could come in, but she didn't close the door either.

Roxie barged through the entryway, and Gladys didn't object.

Andi quietly joined the others in the living room. The condo built in the nineties sported a décor inspired by the eighties. Floral wallpaper covered the walls, while mauve-colored tablecloths draped over flimsy circular tables flanked a teal and pink rose-patterned sofa.

After they all sat, Roxie lifted a pair of oversized glasses off one of the tables. The lenses had to be a half-inch thick. "Good grief, girl! You're as blind as a bat."

Gladys snatched them back. "I only need them for reading."

They weren't going to get anywhere if Roxie kept annoying her.

"Gladys," Andi began. "I wanted to make sure you were okay after last night."

"Yes," Roxie said, shooting Andi a glare. "*We* wanted to make sure you weren't doing anything you might regret after your meltdown last night."

"I'm sorry." Gladys sniffled and struggled to regain her composure. "I guess it was a meltdown. I couldn't help it. I don't want to move back to Ohio and not just because of the weather. Don't get me wrong, I love my family, but my daughter has five sons. Have you ever watched over five boys under the age of ten?"

Andi shook her head while memories of boys playing kickball on the playground flashed through her mind. Meanwhile, Roxie's expression said she would rather walk across hot coals than babysit five boys.

"When I visit," Gladys continued, "my daughter makes up excuses to leave the house. And not just once in a while, it's every single day. Believe me, I understand the need to escape. One time, the boys played cops and robbers and tied me to a chair. They left me like that for two hours! I can't live in that house! Not to mention my daughter treats me like I'm incapable of making my own decisions. She even orders for me at restaurants. I don't want to eat kale. Nobody really likes kale! I don't care if French fries will harden my arteries. I've lived a long time. I deserve to eat anything and everything I want."

"I won't touch kale," Roxie whispered.

"I get it," Andi said. "You wanted Betsy to tell you how she made her money so you could pay off your debt and remain in your own home."

Gladys nodded. "I would do anything to stay in my home."

Roxie narrowed her eyes. "Even commit murder?"

"I didn't do it! I swear!" Gladys's scream contorted her face. She looked like a ghastly Halloween character.

"Then why did we find this in front of your condo?" Roxie tried to whip the butterfly necklace out of her bra, but it got stuck. She yanked harder and almost fell over when it finally came free. While holding up the shiny necklace, she winced and rubbed at the scratch mark near her neck.

"Is that the murder weapon?" A river of tears slid down Gladys's cheeks.

"No." Andi shook her head. *She has no clue what happened to Betsy.* "I'm sorry we disturbed you. We'll see ourselves out." She wanted to give Roxie a piece of her mind once they made their way clear of the condo, but then something caught her eye. A picture in a shadow box hanging on the wall showed a much younger Gladys on stage dressed as Scarlett O'Hara. Andi stepped closer, thinking maybe it was a photo of Gladys's daughter, but the playbill in the box read Gone with the Wind, Davenport High 1954.

Roxie noticed the shadow box, as well. "Gladys!"

"You should rest." Andi pulled the troublemaker outside before she could accuse Gladys of murder again.

Once the door closed behind them, Roxie shook her hand free. "What's with the bum's rush?"

"I didn't want you to complete the sentence you were forming back there." Andi glanced at the condo, making sure the door remained closed. "We can get more information out her later if she thinks we're on her side."

Roxie scowled. "*Are you* on her side?"

"Not exactly," Andi admitted. "I was feeling sorry for her until I realized she was an actress. Staring in a high school play doesn't prove she's a good actress, but it means she might be able to make us believe a lie."

Roxie narrowed her eyes. "Gladys cannot be trusted."

****

They continued down the road toward the pool. Andi wanted to talk to Roxie's water aerobics group called The Water Guppies. Betsy had been a member for years. They would know if she had any enemies, and hopefully, they would talk. Roxie wasn't helpful at all.

Andi was about to turn down the path to the pool when she noticed a white van parking in front of the clubhouse. "Pestbusters." The magnetic sign on the passenger door was an amusing spin on the movie title *Ghostbusters.*

"That must be Poppy's cousin," Roxie said. "Let's go get a look at him. Poppy's a cutie, so he's probably hot."

"And probably young."

"No one over the age of twenty is too young for me." Roxie swung her bony hips as she walked down the path.

"Hold on." Andi caught up in two strides. "Answer me one question—truthfully."

"If I must." Her expression said she didn't want to answer anything.

"Why didn't you fall all over Mack during the baking lesson? He's a handsome guy."

Roxie sighed. "If you must know, I was doing a good deed."

Andi lifted a brow.

"I picked him out for Meg," Roxie explained. "I like her, even if she's usually as hyper as a Chihuahua. The three of us went through a lot during the neighborhood war. We sort of bonded, and I think Meg did a good thing focusing on raising her son for all those years. Now that he's all grown up, she deserves a stud to tango in the sheets with all night long."

"Ahh, Roxie, you *are* a softy." Andi felt her smile widen and her heart warm. "I knew it all along."

"Don't go ordering a halo for me yet. That was my one good deed for the decade."

Andi let the comment go unanswered as her gaze followed the dark-haired man stepping around the van. She raised her voice. "You must be Poppy's cousin."

"That's me! I'm John Nix, ma'am." Although his hair wasn't the same color as his cousin's, it did have the same natural curl. His mustache and sexy beard stubble made him Hollywood handsome. A light tan uniform protected his clothing, while a brown patch with his name embroidered in white thread confirmed his name was John. "I hear you have an ant problem. We use an all-natural formula that won't harm pets but will have your bugs heading for the hills or the complex next door to yours."

"All-natural is good." Andi hoped all-natural was going to be strong enough to get rid of their ants. The pesticide the other company used was useless and smelled horrible.

He handed her his business card designed with a cartoon picture of a bug zapped by a Ghostbusters-type trap. "This visit is a favor for my cousin. I'll spray your clubhouse inside and out for free. If you like our work and decide you want to hire us, give me a call, and we can arrange a time for me to come back out to spray the rest of the complex."

Roxie pulled the board's extra key to the clubhouse out of her bra and looked at him like a predator. "I'll let you inside."

Andi was once again amazed and terrified by everything the woman stored under her clothing.

"John, thank you for coming out. Roxie, I'll meet you at the pool. I'm going to talk to The Water Guppies." Before leaving, Andi leaned closer to her and whispered, "Don't scare him. I want those ants gone."

Roxie waved her off. "You worry too much."

John might face scary creatures for a living, but Andi doubted he ever had to deal with anything like a geriatric cougar before. Roxie didn't care that their age difference was probably a number larger than his actual age.

Andi took several steps and then glanced back at Poppy's cousin, removing his equipment from the back of his van. Part of her wanted to run to his rescue, but in her heart, she knew Roxie was more bark than bite.

Female voices and laughter drifted from the pool area. While Andi opened the gate, she breathed in the heavy scent of chlorine. Three of The Water Guppies stood around a patio table, huddled over a plastic pitcher of strawberry margaritas—their signature drink—and a tube of red disposable cups. None of them came dressed for water aerobics.

"No exercising today?" Andi asked. The water sprayed by the aerator created the only movement in the pool. Droplets landed on the surface at the deep end, producing circles that spread out into bigger ones until they collided with the surrounding tiles.

"We canceled the class to take time to grieve." Lorraine, a grandma with gray hair and rosy cheeks, who could play Mrs. Santa Claus in any movie or play, poured the red liquid into a cup and handed it to her.

Andi didn't bother asking if ten o'clock was too early for alcohol. The Water Guppies drank anywhere and at any hour. Usually, there were at least a half dozen of them splashing around and drinking together. "Where's the rest of your group?"

"They're on a Caribbean cruise," Martha said before taking a sip. At first glance, she appeared more sophisticated than her friends. She had sleek, straight hair that curled under her delicate jawline, and her flowing khaki-colored dress with a geometric design must have come from a boutique store. "I don't swim."

What? "But you're in a water aerobics group?"

Martha smiled. "I sit on the stairs and kick my legs. We're more of a sunbathing, social group."

"She wears water wings." Irene, a spunky grandma with long hair, crossed her legs, which were covered by a mid-length, multi-colored sundress. She lifted her cup to her thin lips layered with shiny gloss but paused to add, "I, on the other hand, swim fifty laps a day. It's how I stay fit and trim."

Lorraine giggled, making her look even more like Mrs. Claus.

Irene frowned. "What's so funny?"

Lorraine's apple cheeks turned red. "I heard it's your favorite night-time exercise that keeps you thin."

Irene's expression turned serious, and then she shrugged. "That, too."

Andi must have looked confused because Lorraine explained, "Irene has three boyfriends."

"Ohh." Andi turned to Irene. "Congratulations?"

"Thank you." Irene turned to Lorraine. "That was a secret, remember?"

"Sorry." Lorraine hung her head low.

"Just don't tell anyone else." Irene held her cup high. "Enough about me, we should toast to Betsy."

"Hold on! I'm coming!" Roxie pushed the gate open and then took her time crossing the pool decking.

She didn't have the pep and cheer of a woman who had snagged a hot young man, so Andi guessed she'd struck out with the bug guy. Roxie needed to stick to men her own age like The Cowboy. One day, he would figure out they were a good match.

Martha filled a cup with the red liquid and handed it to Roxie. "Here you go."

"Since I'm the founding member of The Water Guppies, I'll give the toast." Roxie took a sip before holding her cup high. She waited until the last cup was lifted to speak. "Betsy was a nice woman who should have kept a gun under her pillow like I do. A very big gun."

Martha coughed. "What Roxie is trying to say is, Betsy was a good friend, a nice lady, and a bit careless."

The others nodded.

Andi felt her eyebrows knit together. *Guns? Careless? This is the strangest toast I've ever heard.*

"We'll miss you, Betsy." Unshed tears welled in Irene's eyes. "You were a great movie buddy. Whenever I didn't want to watch a scary film alone, you always agreed to come over."

"And she brought the popcorn," Lorraine added. "It

always had just the right amount of butter."

"It needed more salt," Roxie said. "But she had high blood pressure, so I let it slide."

"That was big of you," Andi said, trying her best not to sound sarcastic.

"I'm that kind of person." Roxie gulped her drink. "Enough gushing. I'm not wearing waterproof mascara." The woman's lashes were so thick her face would look like tar pits if her mascara ran.

Andi remembered she'd come for a specific reason. "Can any of you tell me how Betsy acquired her recent wealth?"

"Gambling," they all said in an obviously rehearsed chorus.

"Where?" Andi expected another coached answer.

Their voices overlapped.

"Horse races."

"Vegas."

"Ostrich races."

"Bingo."

"All of the above," Roxie said matter-of-factly. She glared at Irene as if warning her not to talk. The petite woman, who was the chattiest of the group, furrowed her brow. She didn't appreciate the message.

Asking them about the money wasn't getting Andi anywhere, so she chose a new approach. "Roxie asked me to find Betsy's killer. I need your help, ladies. You were her friends. You knew her better than anyone else." She watched them look down or away, hopefully out of guilt and not avoidance. "Did she have any enemies?"

"Enemies?" Lorraine repeated. "She mentioned a girl named Heather calling her names."

"That was in first grade," Martha said.

Andi wanted to sigh. "Anything more recent?"

"Gladys." Roxie swallowed a gulp of her drink and then wiped her lips with the back of her hand. "Gladys was her enemy."

"Gladys wouldn't leave her alone," Martha said. She ran her perfectly polished nails around the tip of her cup. "I told Betsy it was a mistake to flaunt her good fortune. It attracts attention."

Andi turned to Roxie. "Show them the necklace."

She frowned but relented. After a minute of patting her chest and glancing down inside of her jumpsuit, she removed the silver butterfly.

"That's Betsy's!" Martha reached for it, but Roxie held it back.

"See the small accent diamonds?" Irene pointed to the wings. "That is what makes it memorable. I was with Betsy when she bought the necklace. She wanted something to go with her new dress. We must have gone to six jewelry stores that day."

"I found it in front of Gladys's condo," Roxie said smugly.

"No!" Irene's jaw dropped. "That's all the evidence I need. She's guilty!"

"The police will need more than a necklace found in front of a building connecting eight condos." Andi hoped The Water Guppies would give Gladys the benefit of the doubt until there was more proof found. "Anyone could have dropped the necklace while walking over the grass. Can you describe any other unique pieces of jewelry Betsy owned? If the police find those pieces inside someone's property, that will go a long way in proving who killed her."

"Unique?" Martha shrugged. "My memory isn't what it used to be."

"Betsy liked to make jewelry when she was bored," Irene said. "Her favorite necklace was a silver dolphin charm hanging from a string of blue, glass beads."

"That was pretty," Lorraine said. "I also remember she had a bracelet made from real shells she found on the beach in California. I don't know how she kept them from breaking."

Andi turned to Roxie. "Do you remember seeing those items last night?"

She pressed her cup against her temple as she thought for a moment. "No, they weren't there. The killer has to be Gladys. What burglar would steal homemade jewelry when there was a perfectly good television to swipe?"

Who would steal a seashell bracelet? Andi turned

when she heard the gate open again.

"You were discussing Betsy's jewelry?" Detective Franks appeared to study them as he approached. Andi remembered the no-nonsense detective from her sister's days at the police station. He always sent a disapproving glare her way whenever he saw her. If you weren't at the station to help him with his case, you were in his way and should leave.

"I'm glad you're here, Detective Franks," Andi said, stretching the truth a bit. "We were about to call you." She ignored his expression of doubt as she noticed his plaid hat looked like a modern version of something Sherlock Holmes might wear. Sherlock would have considered her a nuisance as well.

Roxie held up the necklace. "I found this in front of Gladys's condo and *just learned* that it belonged to Betsy."

"*Just learned*, huh?" He frowned at her while he removed an evidence bag from the breast pocket of his jacket, and then held it under the necklace. "Drop it in."

For once, Roxie followed a direction without mouthing off.

"I'll need you to come to the station," he told her.

"Why? I didn't do anything!"

"That's right," Lorraine said with a twinkle in her eye similar to one Santa would have. "She didn't have a motive to kill Betsy. Roxie has her own money. A ton of it!" She snapped her mouth shut as if realizing she'd let something slip that she should have kept private.

Andi wished Lorraine would have continued. She might have given them a clue to solving the murder.

"You have a ton of money?" Detective Franks arched a thick, graying brow.

"Roxie sold her business when she retired and invested in the stock market," Martha explained, sounding like a financial planner.

"Best hair salon in town!" Roxie patted her mint-green hairdo. "I can make you look like any celebrity. Dolly Parton was my specialty."

He blinked several times as though trying to erase the mental picture of Roxie turning him into Dolly. "I want you to come to the station for fingerprinting. I'm going to have to dust the charm on the necklace for prints, and we'll want to eliminate yours from any potential suspects."

"Oh, that's all," Roxie said. "You already have my prints. Search for Roxie Blackwell on your computer."

Andi shouldn't have been surprised, but she was.

"I used to protest when I was younger," Roxie said casually. "It was a sixties thing. We all did it."

Andi scratched her forehead. "In Phoenix?"

"Yes, Phoenix." Roxie gave her an incredulous look. "Nixon flew into Sky Harbor, and a large group of us stood at the fence and held signs protesting the Vietnam War."

"And they arrested you?" That was news to Andi.

"Protesting?" Lorraine chuckled. "Is that what they call it when you take off your bra and throw it at the president?"

"They arrested her because it was so big they thought she was trying to kill the commander in chief with a flying projectile." Irene fell over laughing.

The detective caught the spunky grandma with the glossy lips before she hit the pool decking. He eased her back up, and she batted her eyelashes at him.

Andi hid her smile behind her hand.

Detective Franks cleared his throat and stepped back quickly. "Mrs. Blackwell, don't leave town."

Andi watched him go, and once she was sure he was out of hearing distance, she turned back to The Water Guppies. "Are you ladies going to tell me what's really going on here?"

"Roxie's bra is a deadly weapon," Martha said. "With everything she keeps in there, the FBI could have considered her throwing it at Nixon an act of terrorism even if she did miss him by two hundred yards."

The Water Guppies giggled.

"You know that's not what I'm talking about," Andi said. "Are you going to tell me how Betsy got her money?"

Roxie met her gaze. "Do you want to be an accessory after the fact?"

"Of course not."

"There's your answer." Roxie downed the rest of her

margarita.

****

How do they expect me to help if they keep throwing up roadblocks? It's not like I asked them to let me investigate. Roxie begged me to find Betsy's killer. Andi felt the tension building in her forehead as she marched away from the pool area. She kept walking toward the road, one foot after another, but she had no clue what she should do next. She was too frustrated to focus.

Then, like the answer to a prayer, she spotted her boyfriend, Luke, driving the complex's golf cart to complete his rounds. He had been the property manager for Euphoria Lane long before she moved to the complex.

Just seeing him made her feel better. When she reached the curb, she jerked her thumb over her shoulder to imitate a hitchhiker.

"Going my way?" She batted her eyelashes at him, and he swerved to a stop in front of her.

"Anywhere you're going—I'm going." He patted the seat next to him and shot her a smile that made her heart flutter.

"I am so glad to see you!" she said as she jumped on. She tried her best to keep her negative emotions from showing. He didn't need to hear her laundry list of grievances. All she wanted to do was spend some time chatting about a whole lot of nothing, which would allow her to release her irritations and refocus on the case.

"Your face is smiling," he said, "but the throbbing vein at your temple is telling me you're having a rough morning. Spill it."

She looked into his warm, chocolate-colored eyes. "You know me too well." She drew in a deep, calming breath. "That woman is driving me nuts. She refuses to give me a straight answer."

"You must be referring to Roxie." A slight breeze ruffled his thick, sandy-brown hair, and he used his fingers to comb the stray strands back into place.

"Yes, Roxie." *So much for not bothering him with the*

details. "She's ordered the other Guppies not to tell me how Betsy made her money. I'm afraid they are all up to their tiny necks in something they can't handle—something illegal."

"So, quit. If Roxie is going to keep secrets, you can't be expected to investigate on her behalf."

Andi held onto the cart as he left the curb and accelerated. "I know I *should* quit, but if I do, the police will look into Betsy's finances. I'm afraid they might find incriminating evidence that could land our other neighborhood grandmas in prison."

"If The Water Guppies did commit a crime," he said as he veered the cart to the right to avoid an oncoming car, "and that's a big IF, don't you think that will happen regardless of whether or not you help?"

"I may be deluding myself, but I'm hoping I can manage to hand the guilty person over to the police with only the evidence they need to convict him, or her, of murder. If everything is tied up in a neat, tidy bow, they may not need to do any further investigating."

His expression turned severe, and he pulled over to the curb. "What if you find evidence against The Water Guppies? Are you going to keep it from the police? You know that's a crime. I don't want you locked up with a bunch of women who think drinking strawberry margaritas in a pool qualifies as exercise."

"Honestly? I'm not sure what I will do if I find real evidence against them. Could you call the police on a woman who looks and often acts like Mrs. Santa Claus? She even gave me a jar filled with hot chocolate ingredients for Christmas. I was almost convinced she was the real deal. I looked behind her for a jolly man in a red suit, sitting inside of a sled."

"She gave me the same jar. I loved the teeny, tiny marshmallows." A twinkle lit his eyes. "No, I guess you can't throw her in prison. You would end up on the naughty list for the rest of your life."

"And I would deserve it!"

He placed his hands back on the steering wheel, and just when she thought the situation couldn't get any worse, his smile fell away—again. "What if they're smuggling drugs?"

"Bite your tongue!"

"It happens," he said. "Roxie knows some shady characters, and most of The Water Guppies are on fixed budgets. Remember that grandma who taped packages of drugs to her body and smuggled them across the Nogales border?"

"Of course, it was all over the news."

"She had big financial troubles and felt like she had no choice but to do something drastic."

Andi's mind flashed back to her recent conversations with The Water Guppies. Only one of them seemed the type to turn to drug smuggling. "Roxie could carry ten kilos of heroin in that bottomless bra of hers."

"Scary thought." He rubbed his square jaw. "An even scarier thought is they could be the bottom rung of a ladder that goes straight up to an actual drug cartel."

"I cannot begin to tell you how much I hope The Water Guppies aren't messed up in smuggling," Andi said. "Even Roxie would be in over her head."

"I know this is just a theory, but Arizona is close to the border, and you do suspect criminal activity that pays a lot of money."

"And?" She had a feeling she knew what he would say next.

"*And* I *want* to suggest that you wait until your sister comes back from her vacation to make your next move, but I know you won't." Luke reached out and took her hand. "Your natural instinct is to protect the people you care about. Just promise me you won't take any foolish risks."

She nodded. "I promise." Her sister had the police experience, but Andi had already proven she could handle a murder case by herself. "I don't know if it will make you feel any better, but I have been practicing my self-defense moves every day. It's part of my morning routine."

He frowned. "It will make me feel better if you never have to defend yourself."

"I second that." The last thing she wanted was a battle with a killer.

"Do you want me to drop you off at your condo," he said, "or do you want to go on my rounds with me?"

"A ride in the fresh air sounds like a good idea. It might clear my mind."

"Hold on!" He swerved back into the middle of the road. "One mind clearing coming up!"

Andi grinned, feeling much better than she had a half-hour earlier.

Once they reached the other side of the property, they heard yelling.

"Up ahead!" Andi pointed to two young women, standing in a driveway next door to Lorraine's condo. Even from three buildings away, it was apparent they were raging mad.

Luke parked the golf cart in an empty driveway, and they both climbed out.

"You keyed my car!" Emma screeched. Andi recognized the cute blonde, using her cell phone to snap photos of a two-foot-long scratch on the passenger door of a silver-colored compact car. The curvy young woman, wearing designer fashions from head-to-toe, was renting her home from one of the California investors who had recently swooped in to purchase as many of the condos as they could get their hands on.

"I did not!" Nina, an attractive, petite brunette who looked down to earth in jeans and a pale-blue shirt, crossed her hands over her chest. She lived in a condo owned by her parents. "And you can't prove I did," she said, holding her car key in a guilty-looking manner.

"Tell it to the judge!" Emma took another picture before rushing over to Andi's side. "You're the HOA president, do something! Lock her up!"

Lock her up? "We don't have an HOA jail," Andi said.

"You have a supply closet at the pool." Emma sneered at her adversary. "That will do nicely."

"No, it won't!" Luke stepped in between them. "Someone tell us what is going on here."

"She stole my boyfriend," Nina said. "And now she's harassing me with hang-up phone calls."

"It's not my fault if you can't keep your man." Emma

tilted her nose up into the air. "And she's the one making harassing phone calls, not me. She breathes into the phone like a horse having an asthma attack and then hangs up."

Nina waved her fist in the air. "You liar!"

"Ladies," Luke said. He turned to Emma. "Can you prove she keyed your car?"

Emma glared at Nina and then reluctantly whispered, "No."

Nina grinned like a Cheshire cat.

Luke sighed. "Believe me, there is no man worth fighting over, ladies."

Andi winked at him. She'd fight for him.

He sent her his *I'm-trying-to-work* look and then turned back to Emma. "I'm sorry, there is nothing the HOA can do about your car." He glanced at Nina. "But I can do something about you both breaking the HOA rule against excessive noise. You can't be yelling at each other like this. If you don't want to end up with fines, I suggest you stay away from each other."

"Gladly!" Nina stomped off.

"I'm filing a police report!" Emma yelled at her retreating form.

"You do that!" Nina tossed back over her shoulder, then turned her nose up in the air and walked away.

"Thanks for nothing!" Emma snapped at Andi and Luke before marching off to her front door.

Luke sighed. "We haven't heard the end of this."

"I know." Andi patted him on the back. "Let's finish that relaxing ride you promised me."

He rolled his eyes.

Ten minutes later, Luke had checked the pond aerator, the state of the landscaping, signs of broken sprinklers, and any rule violations, then drove back to the clubhouse. Before Andi could jump off the golf cart, she spotted Mack, their new neighbor. His pool attire, along with the multi-colored beach towel he carried over his shoulder, made his destination obvious.

"Mack!" Andi waved. "I want you to meet Luke, the property manager."

"And her *boyfriend*," Luke said, his expression clearly

saying what he did not. *Don't leave that part out.*

Andi pressed her lips down on her smile. She hadn't thought to include that tidbit of information because The Water Guppies made a point of telling every new neighbor. Apparently it was big gossip that the HOA president was dating the property manager.

Mack stepped forward and offered his hand to Luke. "I thought I would join The Water Guppies at the pool. I've never attempted water aerobics before, but I'm sure if anyone can teach me the basics, it's that group. They certainly have a zest for life."

Andi's heart sank again. "They canceled the class. One of The Water Guppies passed away last night," she said, not wanting everyone to know Betsy was murdered.

Mack's expression turned somber. "I'm sorry to hear that."

"They're drinking a toast to her at the pool." Andi could hear The Water Guppies giggling in the distance and imagined they were sharing funny memories of their adventures with Betsy. "If you still plan to go swimming, I hope you like strawberry margaritas. They'll insist you join them for their second and third pitchers of toasting."

He blinked and then apparently caught on that The Water Guppies were going to be drinking for a while. "I'll give my condolences and then perhaps do a few laps in the pool." He patted a small bulge in his stomach. "Retirement hasn't been good to my waistline." He turned to Luke and waved. "It was nice to meet you."

Andi waited until he had walked away to say, "He seems like an okay guy."

"He has no idea what he's walking into," Luke said. "Those women have a way of making a man feel like a lost gazelle trapped in the middle of a pride of lions."

"Mack might be the one man to survive a meeting with The Water Guppies without feeling traumatized."

Luke lifted a brow.

"Roxie has claimed Mack for Meg." Andi couldn't believe she'd just said that. *Can you claim a person for someone else?*

"How does Meg feel about being paired off without her

41

blessings?"

"If she knew about it, she would be giving Roxie a piece of her mind even though I think she secretly might like the idea. She got tongue-tied when they met at the baking lesson. I have never seen her act that way around a man before."

"Interesting," Luke said. "I hope it works out."

THREE

Later that afternoon, Andi carried three plastic shopping bags into the dining room and placed them down on top of her oak table. Before she could unpack her new purchases, the doorbell rang.

She didn't bother peering through the peephole. She knew who would be waiting for her when she tugged open the door, and she was correct. "Hi! I half expected you to call and tell me you would be late because you picked up an extra shift again."

Meg had swapped out her nurse's uniform for jeans and a colorful top. "I need a break from the hospital." The proof showed in her tired eyes. "Plus, you said you needed my help."

"Do you want to take a nap before we tackle this? I don't mind waiting."

"No, I'm fine." Meg followed her into the dining room. "You didn't say much on the phone. What is this about possible smugglers and cameras?"

"Camera, singular—for now." Andi waved her toward the table. "I want to document anyone coming in and out of the complex, so I bought this." She removed the fake turtledove she'd found on sale at the craft store.

Meg reached for it. "Cute! Are you making a Ten Days of Christmas display?"

"Wait for it..." Andi removed a birdhouse from one bag and a box with a spycam from another. "We are going to figure out how to put this camera into that bird."

"And that bird into this house," Meg concluded. "And then what?"

"We're going to hang it from a tree branch directly across from the front gate. We'll start with the one camera since that is all I feel comfortable charging to the agency without my sister's permission. Hopefully, one is all we'll need."

Meg opened one end of the box containing the birdhouse made of light, natural wood. "What if the killer walks onto the property from the golf course or jumps over the wall?"

"I'm afraid I would need a lot more cameras if that turns out to be the case."

"How many?"

"One for every Water Guppy." Andi grimaced.

"What do you mean, one for every Water Guppy? What's going on here?"

Andi eased onto a chair and waited for Meg to do the same before explaining. She wanted to give the conversation the seriousness it warranted. "I'm not positive, but after speaking with Roxie, Irene, Martha, and Lorraine this morning, and watching how they evaded my questions, I have reason to believe The Water Guppies are involved in something illegal, something that has taken a turn for the worse. The first thing that came to Luke's mind was drug smuggling."

Meg slowly blew out a deep breath. "That would explain how Betsy came into so much money and was unwilling to tell anyone a thing about how she got it."

Andi gave a weak shrug. "It would also explain why someone murdered her. Those guys don't play nice. If you cross them in any way, you can forget planning your next birthday party."

"Do you think she took money that didn't belong to her?"

Andi couldn't say for sure, but she did have her suspicions. "She didn't seem like the type, but what do I know? Betsy was more than a little upset when she left the baking lesson. I was thinking she might have gone home and called whoever is in charge to tell him she was quitting."

Meg's eyes widened. "So the cookie left on her chest was a message to the other Guppies to keep their mouths shut and follow orders?"

"That's my biggest fear." Andi studied the fake bird, looking for the best place to cut a hole. "If Luke's guess is correct, there's a chance that one of their thugs may come here to threaten The Water Guppies in person. By placing the camera near the gate, I can look for anyone I don't recognize and record their license plate."

Meg paused. "You don't think any of The Water Guppies could have killed Betsy, do you?"

They stared at each other for a moment, and then they both said, "Noo."

"They would never," Andi said.

"You're right. Let me see the bird." Meg reached out her hand. "I can probably figure out how to plant the camera inside."

After she handed it over, Andi grabbed a step stool from the kitchen and leaned it up against the front door. Next, she found a pair of scissors, strong glue, and a sharp knife, and then placed them on the table. "While you operate on our prop, I'll figure out how the camera works." She removed the directions from the box and began reading. Five minutes later, she looked up. "Seems simple enough."

Meg inserted the camera and aligned the lens with the opening she had created in one of the bird's dark eyes. "Not bad if I say so myself."

"I'll have to start calling you Doc." Andi glued the bird inside of its new home. "Normally, you're supposed to paint the birdhouse, but I don't want it to stand out in the tree."

"Will it stand out because it's not painted?" Meg asked.

"I guess we'll find out." Andi handed over their finished project. "If you take this, I'll carry the step stool."

On their way out the front door, Andi glanced down

and discovered a line of ants traveling over her welcome mat. "Seriously!"

Meg frowned. "You should call Poppy's cousin."

Andi sighed and shifted the handle of the step stool to her shoulder to make it easier to manage. "He does good work. I dropped by the clubhouse earlier, and there was no sign of any ants. Plus, he seems like a nice guy, and I like the fact he uses all-natural products."

"Sounds like you're sold on him." Meg lifted a brow. "Is he cute?"

"I thought you had a thing for our new neighbor?" Andi locked the front door after they exited and turned in time to catch Meg blushing.

"Who?" Meg asked, feigning innocence.

Andi laughed. "Nice try. You got so tongue-tied when Mack walked in the door, I began to wonder if you were having a heart attack or a stroke." She fell into step beside her friend as they walked down the sidewalk toward the trees across from the main gate. "I have to admit I was surprised by your reaction to him."

"Me, too," Meg admitted. "I can't even remember the last time I looked twice at a guy. I didn't want to think about dating after my ex cheated and lied to me. Over the years, I have been so busy working and raising Chad I never missed having a romantic relationship. But now my son is an adult, and he's not home much."

"And then Mack walked in the door," Andi said.

"And then Mack walked in the door," Meg repeated. "I took one look at him and felt like someone had knocked the breath out of me. I have never seen a more handsome man, and suddenly, dating didn't seem impossible any longer."

"This is the perfect time in your life to start dating again."

Meg sighed. "But I blew it. You saw how I acted. Mack must think I'm a silly fool."

"I wouldn't say that." Andi lifted the ladder off her shoulder and held it in front of her. "I could tell he was impressed when he heard you were a nurse."

"At least my occupation proves I have an I.Q. above five." Meg pointed to a large pine up ahead. "That is probably the fullest tree. The Cottonwoods won't provide much cover."

"Good point. We don't want anyone to get a good look at our bird."

"While I prepped her for her undercover assignment, I decided we should call her Vera after a World War II spy."

Andi smiled. "You named a fake bird?"

"There is a method to my madness." Meg stood beneath the tree and waited for her. "If the bird has a name, you won't have to worry about accidentally giving away the fact you have a spy at the gate. You can simply say we should check on Vera."

Andi positioned the step ladder up against the tree trunk and detected the unmistakable aroma of pine. It reminded her of family Christmases she'd celebrated with her parents and three sisters while growing up. Life was so carefree back then. She'd never known anyone who later died at the hands of a murderer. She spotted a neighbor driving out of the gate and released her childhood memory to focus on the present. "What if someone asks who Vera is?"

"You can say she's a friend who had surgery. You'd only be stretching the truth a little."

"I admit, there may be a time when having a nickname for the bird could come in handy." Andi climbed the ladder's three steps. "What if someone asks where she had the surgery performed?"

"Hmm. I know, tell them she doesn't talk about it. It wouldn't be a lie." Meg handed her the birdhouse with a smug expression on her face. "Can you reach that branch?"

"Need some help?" Mack stepped out of the shadows near the side of the clubhouse.

Andi jolted. *Oh, great! He probably heard our entire conversation. How did we not see him?*

"Where did you come from?" Meg studied the area filled with trees and bushes beyond where he stood.

"That way." He gestured back over his shoulder with his thumb. "I helped Martha install a new faucet, and I was heading home between the buildings when I noticed you might need some help."

Act nonchalant. The last thing Andi wanted to do was arouse suspicion. "Thanks. We appreciate the help." She stepped off the ladder to allow him access. "That was nice of you to help Martha."

"It was nothing. I have too much idle time on my hands." He stood on the top step and reached his hand out for the birdhouse.

Andi pried the house from Meg's fingers and then turned it around to make sure the opening faced the gate. Glancing up, she pointed to a spot on the branch that would provide an unobstructed view of the road for the camera and yet was high enough to keep the neighbors from getting a good view of Vera. "How about right there? What do you think, Meg?"

"That's a great spot," she said, her voice cracking on the last word.

When he lifted the birdhouse close to his face, Andi panicked. "So you're a retired dentist. Do you miss your job?"

"Sometimes." He spared a moment to glance down at her. "The transition to retired life would have been easier if I had a hobby."

"Maybe you could answer a question," she said, trying to keep him focused on her and not what he was seeing as he continued his work. "Every time I go to the dentist, he adds to my nightly routine. Did you tell your patients to use an electric toothbrush, followed by floss, then water hosing your gums, rinsing with mouthwash, *and* then rubbing fluoride paste all over your teeth before going to bed? That seems like a lot to do."

He draped the birdhouse's rope loop over a branch and then stepped down off the ladder. "You should talk to your dentist."

"But—"

He waved and left before she could finish her statement.

Andi watched him walk to his condo with long strides. "You know, for a guy who has too much time on his hands, he suddenly seemed in a hurry to leave. I wonder why."

Meg glanced up at the tree. "Do you think he spotted

the camera inside the bird?"

"I don't know," Andi said. "I hope not."

****

An hour later, Andi knocked on Lorraine's condo door, which looked like the other hundred and ninety-nine doors in the complex. She stood still, straining to hear any noise coming from inside.

Meg shifted her weight back and forth on her white tennis shoes. "I don't think she's home."

Andi pressed on the doorbell while noticing how the entire building seemed deserted. The closest neighbor's car wasn't in the driveway, and the condos upstairs belonged to The Water Guppies who went away on a cruise.

Meg glanced over her shoulder as if making sure they were still alone. "What makes you think Lorraine will tell you what The Water Guppies have been up to?"

"She's the weak link. At the pool, she let it slip that Irene is dating three guys."

"Three?" Meg rolled her eyes. "I'm so out of practice I can barely talk to one."

"You could always ask Mack out and practice on him." Andi pressed on the doorbell again. "On second thought—don't. Not until I'm positive he's not the murderer."

"What?" Meg's brows drew together, and her mouth fell open. "You think he might be guilty?"

"I don't know what to think, except that Lorraine is not home." Andi turned to find Roxie headed their way. The woman's mint-green hair and dark sunglasses reminded her of chocolate-mint ice cream.

Roxie eyed them suspiciously. "What are you two up to?"

"No good." Meg glanced at Andi and shrugged.

"We're up to nothing," Andi said. "Lorraine's not home."

"Sure, she is." Roxie tapped on the door. "We have dinner plans." She'd changed into a bright floral jumpsuit and cherry-red stilettos, which made a bold statement when combined with her hair color. She waited a few seconds, and when no one answered, she twisted the knob. The door opened. "Lorraine!"

Andi followed her inside. Halfway through the living room, she caught the smell of rotten eggs. "I think there's a gas leak!"

"Try not to breathe it in." Meg quickly scanned the room. "Lorraine!"

"She takes a nap every afternoon." Roxie rushed toward the master bedroom, but Meg was faster.

Andi ran to the kitchen and discovered the stove burners had been turned on, but the pilot lights were out. The open oven was in the same condition. She turned off the knobs and then ran to the master bedroom. She found Meg and Roxie trying to carry Lorraine's limp body. "I'll take her arms, Roxie. Please go out front and call nine-one-one."

She took hold of Lorraine's skinny ankles beneath her soft, fleece pajama bottoms, and then Roxie shifted out of the way. Meg, positioned at the other end of her body, carried most of the woman's slight weight. Lorraine looked like a hungover Mrs. Claus after downing a dozen cups of eggnog. If it weren't for the rise and fall of her chest with each breath, Andi would have feared they had arrived too late.

Meg and Andi tried their best to maneuver her out the bedroom door and across the living room. Roxie stood just outside the front door. She spoke to the 9-1-1 dispatcher and stepped out of the way as Andi and Meg carried Lorraine out into the fresh air.

"Across the street," Andi said. "That condo could blow at any second."

"What? You have got to be kidding!" Roxie's jaw dropped and then clamped shut when she pulled the phone closer to her ear. "Not you," she told the dispatcher while she quickly followed her friends.

"Someone rigged the oven and stove to make sure the condo would fill with natural gas. We're lucky we arrived in time to save her," Andi huffed. She followed Meg's lead as they lowered Lorraine to the grass. "There's one more thing," she continued. "I found a bull's eye cookie on the counter with Lorraine's name printed on it with white decorating gel."

Roxie told the dispatcher to send the police. "Someone tried to murder my friend!"

****

Andi rifled through a pile of reading material in the hospital waiting room while Meg and Roxie sat in blue plastic-covered chairs, staring at the tiled floor. With a cooking magazine in one hand and a decorating magazine in the other, she glanced out the window at the darkening sky. A rainstorm passing through the area added to the dreary mood. To make matters worse, the aroma of stale cigarettes Roxie carried with her mixed with the aroma of her cheap perfume and the hand sanitizer Meg kept squeezing into her hands from a small bottle she kept in her pocket. Andi had finally settled on a gossip magazine when a distinguished-looking doctor with a stern expression marched toward them. She held her breath, praying for good news.

He referred to his file before speaking. "Are you Lorraine Knapp's family?"

"I'm her sister," Roxie lied. "Is she going to be okay? Tell it to us straight, Doc."

"I'm Dr. Franklin," he said solemnly. His crisp white lab coat and polished black shoes made it look like he never touched patients or worked up a sweat. "Your sister—"

"Is dead!" Roxie suddenly gripped his arms and threw back her head. "I can tell by that look on your face. She's gone!"

"Mrs. Knapp is...awake," he said calmly, prying Roxie's hands off his body.

"Oh." Roxie stepped back. "Sorry about that, Doc. You had me worried there for a minute."

He met Meg's gaze, and recognition replaced the fear on his face. "Can I speak to you in private?"

"Sure." Meg followed the doctor down the hall. They conversed for a few minutes, and then he escaped into another room.

Andi had tried to read their lips but failed. When Meg returned, she asked, "Did Roxie scare him off?"

"What do you think?" Meg slipped into the chair next to Roxie and spoke directly to her. "There wasn't enough gas in Lorraine's system to affect her, but they did find an overdose of ground-up sleeping pills in a red liquid when they pumped her stomach."

"She took sleeping pills with her margarita?" Andi chose a chair on the other side of Roxie, anticipating the need to calm her if she should flip out on them again.

"More like a smoothie," Meg said.

"No!" Roxie gestured like an umpire calling *safe*. "There is no way she tried to kill herself! Her granddaughter is having a baby. She can't wait to be a great grandmother!"

"I didn't imagine the cookie next to the stove." Andi shook her head. "She didn't do this to herself."

"She made herself a strawberry smoothie every afternoon." Roxie pushed herself up off the chair. "Someone could have slipped the ground-up pills into her glass."

"Or into one of the ingredients she put in her drink," Meg suggested.

Roxie waggled her finger at her. "Lorraine kept her canister of strawberry powder on the kitchen counter. I bet whoever tried to kill her spiked her canister."

The elevator dinged, and when the doors slid open, Detective Franks stepped into the hall. He wore a long raincoat to go with his Sherlock Holmes-type hat. His expression was more severe than the doctor's had been.

Andi cringed. "Why do the men in this hospital look like they're on their way to their own funeral?"

"Roxie has that effect on them," Meg said, trying to lighten the mood.

Roxie narrowed her eyes. "Not funny."

Andi grinned. "You have to admit it was a little funny."

"Ladies," Detective Franks said. "I just spoke to the attending doctor. I'm glad to hear your friend will be okay."

"Thank you." Andi stood and stretched her legs. "We

were just on our way to see her."

"That will need to wait." His gaze traveled over each of them before continuing. "I read the police report, and I have a few questions."

"I didn't touch anything," Roxie said. "Except for the front door."

He smiled. "Anyone else?"

Andi raised her hand like a student in school. "I turned off the stove and oven."

"Andi *Stevenson*, right?" he asked, keeping his focus on her.

"Right. Same last name as my sister." She studied him carefully, but his poker face didn't change. Her sister, Jessie, had worked with this man for years, but he didn't offer his opinion of her either way. "I did notice there was a bull's eye cookie with Lorraine's name on it," Andi said. "We didn't write names on the cookies we made at the baking lesson. I think it might be the killer's calling card."

He blinked but remained silent.

Andi continued. "There was one left on Betsy's body, also. This time, someone left it on the counter beside the stove that was used to try to kill Lorraine."

"You *think* someone tried to kill her," he said. "Leave the police work to the experts."

Andi knew there was no point in discussing the matter with him. She walked away and sat next to Meg, who openly glared at him.

He rubbed the back of his neck. "Did any of you notice anything different, besides the cookie?"

"You mean, besides the aroma of rotten eggs?" Meg asked with attitude.

"I noticed something." Roxie's tone said she didn't think much of him either. "Lorraine kept a jade dragon on a shelf in her living room, and on the way out, I noticed it was gone. Her father gave it to her when she was nine. She would never give it away."

"Maybe she moved it." He appeared to be speaking more to himself than to Roxie. "I'll ask Mrs. Knapp when I go in. I'm afraid your visit with her will have to wait until after I leave. Which room is she in?"

A long silence followed until Meg gave in and pointed toward the corner. "That one."

They remained silent until he closed the door behind him.

"Leave the police work to the experts," Roxie mimicked the detective's words.

Andi rolled her eyes. "They have to say that."

"They don't have to be mean about it," Meg said. "He should be nice to you. Your sister was a police officer. They worked together."

A smile tugged at Andi's lips. "I appreciate you both."

Roxie walked over and patted her on the shoulder. "What are friends for?"

Andi's heart swelled. She never knew the madcap, retired hairdresser considered her a friend.

FOUR

The next day, Andi busily worked on a batch of chocolate brownies. Her nerves had been on edge all morning, making her crave something sweet and chocolaty. She spread the batter into her greased and floured baking pan, then carefully placed it into the preheated oven. After setting the timer for thirty minutes, she realized her craving couldn't wait that long.

The events of the previous day played through her mind as she prepared a large glass of chocolate milk. She hated the fact that she never got to be alone with Lorraine long enough to ask her if she was smuggling drugs. Roxie wouldn't leave her friend's side. Although it was annoying because Andi couldn't ask the tough questions without Roxie running interference, it was also heartwarming to see the tough woman showing her softer side.

A loud knock on the door forced her to stop mentally revisiting the events at the hospital. *Who could that be?* She quickly downed the rest of her milk and then placed the glass in the sink. The knocking became insistent and alternated with doorbell chimes.

"Coming!" *Please do not be an HOA complaint.* No matter how many times she instructed the neighbors to email their grievances to the property management company, they still insisted on telling her all about them.

Once she reached the door, she tugged it open and found Roxie with a young woman she didn't recognize.

"Are you going to let us in?" Roxie asked.

"Of course." Andi stepped back and waved them inside. Roxie and the stranger headed straight for the living room, where they sat on the white linen couch. Andi, suspecting she might be in for a long and serious conversation, eased onto the red accent chair, and then looked directly at Roxie. "What's up?"

She gestured to the woman on her right. "This is Gladys's daughter, Joyce. She flew into town last night."

The thirty-something brunette had inherited her mother's small round face, big eyes, and a small nose. Her jeans and navy-blue, light-weight sweater and flat shoes showed she also had her mother's no-nonsense taste in clothing. "They..." She covered her mouth and pressed back her cry. "They arrested my mother this morning."

"What?!" Andi glanced at Roxie for an explanation. She always knew what was going on in the neighborhood.

"That detective found Betsy's dolphin necklace," Roxie said matter-of-factly. "I was looking through the bedroom window with my opera binoculars when the police searched her condo."

Andi couldn't believe her ears. "You go to the opera?"

"Of course not!" Roxie guffawed. "I wouldn't be caught dead cozying up to those rich stiffs. The binoculars used to belong to my ex-husband. I kept them because you never know when you might need to look through someone else's window, and who wants to carry those heavy ones?" She suddenly waved away the conversation dramatically with both hands. "Once again, you're missing the point."

"They arrested my mother!" Joyce dabbed at her tears. "That's the point! I know she didn't do it. Someone planted that necklace in her jewelry box. My mother is a God-fearing woman. She would never steal."

"You mean she would never commit murder," Roxie said.

"That, too." Joyce met Andi's gaze. "Did you ever see that necklace? The lawyer showed us a picture. It looks like something a child made. My mother would never kill someone and then steal the most hideous thing she could find just so the police could arrest her."

"You have a point." Andi leaned back in the chair and crossed her arms over her chest. "If I were going to frame someone for murder, which I would never do, I would plant something that the victim obviously owned."

Joyce pressed her fingers against her temple. "This is all my fault. I should have never insisted that she move back to Ohio and live with me. I was just so afraid that she would end up in bankruptcy court. Her credit card bill was out of control because she stayed up late, buying useless stuff sold on cable TV. She owed over three hundred dollars!"

"Three hundred dollars?" Andi had expected her to say something closer to three thousand dollars. "How much was she paying per month?"

Joyce hesitated. "One hundred."

Andi tried to wrap her head around this new information. "So her debt would have been paid off in four months if she started going to bed early? Maybe you could have asked her doctor to prescribe sleeping pills."

Joyce threw her hands up in the air. "I know! I'm a terrible daughter! I told her she had to be able to pay it off this month or come live with me. I was selfish. I wanted my mother to come home."

Roxie guffawed. "You wanted her home to babysit your brat pack."

Joyce hid her head in her hands and nodded. "I love my boys, but they are brats. I need help."

"First, you need help getting your mother out of jail," Andi said.

"I know a bail bondsman," Roxie added. "If she makes bail."

At times like this, Andi was grateful for Roxie and all of her connections.

"Thank you both." Joyce turned to Andi. "Roxie already told me you're investigating this case for free."

Andi glared at Roxie. "That isn't something we want widely known."

"I promise not to mention it to anyone else," Joyce

said. "I don't have a lot of money, but if you can prove my mother is innocent before this goes to court, we can pay you something. I'm not sure how much. I'll have to ask my husband."

Andi's heart wanted to tell her to keep her money, that she was glad to help out, but her sister's voice in her head told her they were running a business, not a charity. "I'll do everything I can to clear her name, but I am going to need you to do something for me."

"Anything!" A hint of hope reflected in the unshed tears in Joyce's eyes.

"Betsy's condo is still sealed off. Joyce's lawyer can get me inside—if you make the request."

****

After an hour of conducting internet searches on Betsy and Gladys for any piece of information that might help, Andi tossed out a piece of scratch paper and then stared at her overflowing kitchen trash can. Her sister wouldn't be back for over a week. She had to stop putting off the inevitable. Ever since she'd found a dead body in the dumpster, she tried to avoid the chore.

"No time like the present. It's starting to stink in here." She tugged the bag out and hauled it outside. When she reached the street, she spotted Meg climbing out of her SUV.

"Wait for me!" Meg pushed the driver's side door shut and jogged over. "I'll walk with you."

"You think I can't throw the trash away by myself," Andi said, even though she knew she might chicken out at any minute.

"Call it emotional support." Meg shot her a smile. "I don't blame you for not wanting to go near a dumpster. If I found a dead body in a closet, I would remove the doors off all of my closets and buy extra dressers to hold my clothes."

"And I would admire you for coming up with that clever response to a horrible situation. Let's hope it never happens." Andi shifted the bag to the other hand. It weighed a ton. That was the downfall of waiting too long to complete the simple chore. The closer she got to the dumpster, the faster her heart raced.

"Andi! Andi!" Emma, the blonde who stole her neighbor's boyfriend, ran toward her.

"Get back here!" Nina, the brunette who keyed her car—allegedly—ran after her, although awkwardly in her high heeled boots.

"Not again," Andi whispered.

"What's that all about?" Meg asked, just as the two young women caught up to them.

Emma pointed at Nina. "She left a burning bag of dog poop on my porch!"

"Prove it!" Nina said with a smug expression that expressed her guilt more than words ever could.

"I don't have to." Emma planted her hands on her hips. "I filed for a restraining order, and you are breaking the law by standing here next to me!" She turned to Andi. "You are both witnesses." She then removed her cellphone from her pocket and began recording. "Nina is breaking the law by following me to the dumpster."

Nina sneered. "I haven't received a restraining order, so I'm not breaking anything."

"Other than my peace of mind," Meg said.

"And the rule against excessive noise," Andi added. "That's twice now, ladies."

"Aren't you concerned that she could have burned down the complex?" Emma shoved the phone, still recording, in Andi's face.

"Of course I am." She pushed the phone aside. "You two aren't giving me any choice. Nina, I'm going to have to consult with our attorneys. Fire is a serious matter. Emma, I suggest you get some surveillance equipment, like the doorbell with the camera."

"I'm going to get that, too!" Nina pointed her finger in the other girl's face. "She acts like an angel, but remember, she's the one who stole my boyfriend!"

Andi resisted the urge to roll her eyes. "If either of you records any proof, please send me a copy."

"I will!" Emma said as she marched off.

"Me, too!" Nina said as she marched off in the opposite

direction.

Meg sighed and lifted the lid to the dumpster. "The drama never ends around here."

"You're telling me." Andi tossed the bag inside without looking into the dumpster and then began walking away.

"Andi!" Poppy walked at a fast pace toward them.

"I hope it's not another complaint," Meg said.

"I just heard about Gladys." Poppy rubbed the cold from her bare arms when she reached them. The recent rains had dropped the temperature to the high sixties. "Is it true? Was she arrested for Betsy's murder?"

Meg nodded. Andi had called her with the news immediately after Roxie and Joyce had left her condo.

"Wow!" Poppy shook her head. "I know she was mad when Betsy wouldn't tell her how she made her money, but I never dreamed she would kill her."

"We don't think she did," Meg said.

Andi didn't want to give away too much information. "We have a hard time believing anyone in our neighborhood could be a killer."

Meg choked on the absurdity of the comment. Anyone who lived on Euphoria Lane for more than a year knew this wasn't the first time they feared a murderer lived in the complex. It wasn't even the second time.

Andi preferred not to bring up the past, especially to this student who needed to focus on her studies. And just because there had been a murderer in the past didn't mean they had an easy time accepting the fact, so she hadn't lied.

Poppy continued to rub her arms. She should have pulled a sweater on over her T-shirt before running outside to catch up with them. "I heard you work for a private investigator, and Roxie hired you to investigate the case. That is so cool!"

"Roxie didn't hire me," Andi said. There was no money exchanged, so again, she hadn't lied. "I agreed to ask a few questions. Detective Franks, with the police department, is the real investigator."

"Ohh." Poppy looked disappointed. She glanced over her shoulder as if making sure they were still alone. "When you were asking questions, did you find out how Betsy made her money? We could all use some extra cash, right?"

"I'm afraid she's taking her secret to the grave," Andi said.

"Are you sure?" Poppy scanned the area around them again. "Isn't she friends with that exercise group?"

"The Water Guppies?" Meg furrowed her brow. "She is, but I haven't noticed any of them spending a lot of money. If she told anyone, it would have been Lorraine." Meg's jaw dropped as if she suddenly realized why Lorraine had been the second target.

"What?" Poppy studied Meg. "What do you know?"

"Nothing," Andi said. "It's just that Lorraine got sick and ended up in the hospital, but she's coming home today."

"I hope it wasn't anything too serious." Poppy hit herself in the head with the palm of her hand. "Of course it was serious. She went to the hospital. What I meant is I hope it wasn't anything that will continue to cause her problems in the future."

"She'll be fine," Meg said.

"Nothing to worry about." Andi knew the rumor mill would tell the whole complex what had happened, but if she could delay the inevitable for a few days, it might help her with the investigation.

"That's good," Poppy said, but her expression said she was confused, or maybe she was just disappointed that she wasn't learning the secret to Betsy's financial success.

****

Andi tried to relax on her patio chair while she watched Luke grill marinated chicken, but she couldn't get the case off her mind. "I'm afraid I might not be good company tonight."

"You're always good company." He offered a warm smile before shoveling the chicken breasts onto two plates.

She opened the deli container and served them each an extra-large portion of potato salad. The day's events had left her feeling hungry for both food and information. "Thanks for dinner. I owe you one."

His chair made a screeching noise when he scooted closer to the table. "No, you don't. I told you I would prepare most of our meals."

She arched a brow. "Is that a subtle dig at my cooking?"

"Not at all," he said with a good-natured chuckle. "We all know you are a much better baker than you are a cook. I'll leave it at that." He handed her a roll. "Let's discuss what is really on your mind. Do you think Gladys is guilty?"

"I want to say no. I have a hard time believing Gladys is foolish enough to kill Betsy, steal her necklace, and then keep it in her jewelry box where anyone could easily find it."

Luke poured her a glass of lemonade from a pitcher. "Is she claiming the necklace is hers?"

"No, which you would think would be her defense if she stole it." Andi took a bite of her chicken and chewed slowly, trying to determine which ingredients he used in the marinade. "This is good. I admit I can't cook, and that you should always prepare dinner for us."

His face lit up with amusement. He lifted his glass but paused before taking a sip. "It looks to me like the killer framed Gladys."

"That's what I was thinking, but then that means the real killer had to know about their fight at the clubhouse. That shoots a hole in your drug smuggling theory." She filled her fork with potato salad. "They always say to follow the money. I asked Gladys's daughter to get me inside Betsy's house with the defense lawyer. I need to go through her financial documents. She seemed like the type to keep hard copies."

He leaned back in his chair. "There's one thing I don't understand. Why would Roxie ask you to investigate if she knew you would find evidence against her and the other Water Guppies?"

Andi shrugged. "I gave up trying to figure Roxie out a long time ago. She has a way of thinking that is alien to the rest of us."

"Boy, is that the truth!"

After dinner, they booted up her laptop and viewed the

security footage taken by Vera, the fake bird spying from the tree across from the front gate.

"There!" Andi pointed to a security guard, driving a gray truck. "He doesn't live here."

Luke froze the screen, giving them a good view of the driver. "I've seen him park in Lorraine's driveway a few times."

Andi checked the timestamp. "That was a half-hour before we found Lorraine passed out in her condo." She took a picture of the screen and sent it to Lorraine, along with a text. *Do you recognize this man?*

"You may have found your first good lead in this case." Luke leaned over and placed a gentle kiss on her lips. "Are you still going to marry me if you become a famous detective with your own reality TV show?"

She laughed. "Is that a proposal?"

A twinkle lit his eyes as he reached into the pocket of his jacket.

Andi's jaw dropped when she spotted the jewelry box. "What? When did..."

Luke lowered to a bent knee and opened the box to reveal a sparkling, radiant cut diamond ring. "Andi, I love you with all my heart. Will you marry me?"

Tears welled in her eyes. "Yes! I love you with all of my heart, too."

He slid the ring on her finger and pulled her in for another kiss. At that moment, her cell phone chirped to signal an incoming message.

"It can wait," she said as she slid the phone further away on the table and then placed her lips on his with more force this time.

He pulled back from the kiss. "Inquiring minds need to know." He grinned as he grabbed her phone and read the message from Lorraine out loud. "That's my cousin."

"I doubt someone tried to kill Lorraine over a family squabble." She touched his lower lip with her fingertip. "Right now, at this very moment, we should concentrate on us. The investigation can wait until tomorrow."

"True." He pretended to nibble on her finger. "I'm glad you have your priorities straight." He placed his lips on hers but then suddenly pulled back. "Maybe my theory wasn't off base, after all. Her cousin could be a drug smuggler. If he is, that would explain how the killer found out about Gladys's fight with Betsy."

"If you're right, he must have been afraid Lorraine would rat him out to the police for killing Besty." She was about to kiss Luke again when she paused. "I forgot to tell you. Our new neighbor Mack was walking the complex about the time Lorraine's stove was rigged to kill her."

"The dentist?"

"About that, I asked him a simple dental question, and he referred me to my own dentist. I thought that was odd. I wasn't asking for a diagnosis."

"I can look into him for you," Luke said. "I know the guy he's renting from."

"I love you more every day." This time, Andi kissed him the way he deserved—without interruption.

FIVE

Early the next morning, Andi met Gladys's court-appointed lawyer, Blake Ramsey, in front of Betsy's condo. If she had to guess, she would say he was a linebacker in college about thirty years ago. His dark gray suit threatened to split at the seams every time his shoulders shifted. A patch of sweat on his bald head reflected the midmorning sun. The only touch of softness came from a baby-blue colored tie.

"Thank you again," Andi said, meaning every word. He didn't have to agree to let her inside.

"Just don't touch anything without me giving you the okay."

"Got it!" She waited for him to unlock the door. "I'm particularly interested in any documents she might have in her desk."

"We'll check that first." He pushed the door open.

"Wait for me!" Roxie, wearing a sparkly gold jumpsuit and gold stilettos, tip-toe raced down the sidewalk toward them.

Andi stifled a groan.

"Is she with you?" the lawyer asked, looking amused.

"She...works for our agency." The glare Andi sent Roxie warned her to behave.

"I'm here," Roxie said, sounding like a wounded

65

animal as she drew in hoarse-sounding breaths. Her lungs sounded like they were going to collapse at any minute. "Let's get this show on the road."

"Don't touch anything," he ordered again before stepping inside.

Andi stayed behind long enough to whisper, "You might want to rethink the smoking."

"At my age, my body might go into shock if it breathed in clean air."

Andi shook her head in response and then entered the dark condo. Her biggest complaint about the buildings within the complex was the limited number of windows. While searching for a desk, she followed the lawyer as he flipped on the lights connected to ceiling fans. Inside the spare bedroom, they located a mahogany desk in the corner.

She pointed to a leather chair. "Can I sit down?"

He checked his notes. "I don't know what you think you might find, but the detectives already went through everything inside, so you can snoop all you want."

Snoop? Andi hated the way he looked down his nose at her. *He probably doesn't like private investigators.* She swiveled the chair to pull out the largest drawer, careful to avoid the fingerprinting dust. When she lifted a large file labeled BANK, she caught Roxie removing a small book from her bra.

"Look what I found under the bed!" Roxie waved a small book above her head. "I heard Betsy was a big gambler. Now I know the secret to her success."

Andi choked on the words she wanted to say and then coughed them away. If she said anything, they would both get kicked out, and Roxie would end up in a jail cell.

The lawyer frowned. "The police searched under the bed."

Roxie stared him down. "It was *wedged* between the wall and the headboard. With the white cover, *I* can see how they could have missed it."

Andi bit her tongue. She would have it out with Roxie later.

The lawyer hesitated, then cautiously reached for the

book and examined it. "You can buy this at any bookstore. It means nothing. Put it back where you found it."

Roxie narrowed her eyes. "It means—"

"It means nothing," Andi said. "Listen to the man. He's a lawyer."

While Roxie had tried, unsuccessfully, to change the narrative around Betsy's murder, Andi skimmed through Betsy's bank statements. A deposit for ten thousand dollars caught her attention.

"That's from a brokerage firm," the lawyer said, looking over her shoulder. "She must have sold part of her financial portfolio. That isn't unusual for a person her age, living on a fixed income."

Andi found similar deposits in four other statements. "Is that common, too? It looks like she was selling off a lot of stock."

"The recent unpredictability of the market could have spooked her. She wasn't in a position to risk losing money in another recession. Either that or maybe she was expecting the need for more money on hand."

Roxie sidled up to the desk. "Betsy said she needed a new hip."

"That would explain it." Andi hoped the deposits were as innocent as the lawyer thought they were.

Once they were outside and Blake Ramsey had left, Andi turned to Roxie. "What were you thinking? You could go to prison for planting evidence!"

"I didn't know she had stocks. I figured there needed to be a reasonable explanation for where she got her money."

Andi studied the blank expression on the other woman's face. "You don't know where Betsy got her money, do you?"

Roxie shook her head. "No."

"Then what was all that *conspiracy after the fact* talk?"

"I figured Betsy, and maybe even some of the other Guppies, were doing something illegal— but no one would talk. I'm beginning to think they don't know anything either. I guess Betsy did get her money from selling or trading stocks."

Andi ran her hand through her hair. *Then maybe Gladys did kill her. No one else had a motive.*

****

A few hours later, Andi stepped out of the dressing room, feeling like Cinderella. She lifted the hem of the floor-length, lace wedding dress with one hand while trying to close the plunging neckline with the other. Showing too much skin made her feel self-conscious.

Meg's jaw dropped. "You look beautiful!" Her eyes clouded over with unshed tears. "I can't believe you're getting married! How exciting!" She sat on a sofa positioned near the changing rooms and accepted the two glasses of champagne offered by an overly friendly saleswoman. She placed one on the coffee table. "This is for you when you're finished."

"I'll be finished right after I take this dress off. It's the tenth one I've tried on." Andi stepped in front of the three full-length mirrors and glanced down at her bare feet. She couldn't decide if she wanted a long dress or a short one. *I should have gotten a pedicure. Who tries on dresses with ugly toes?*

"You've only tried on ten? That's nothing. This is a marathon, dear friend." Meg took another sip from her fluted glass. "I'm surprised they let us drink near their dresses."

"They're competing with the store down the street, and I'm sure they have a *You ruin it, you buy it,* policy." Andi turned and glanced over her shoulder to study the back of her dress in the mirror's reflection. "I want to narrow my choices down to five before I bring my mother here."

"Have you told her yet?"

"No. You know my mother. She'll insist I come home to their house every evening to start planning the wedding. I want to solve this case first."

"That's a good idea." Meg set down her glass and picked up a pad of paper and pen. "This dress goes in the Show Mom category. It makes you look slim and sexy."

Andi smiled. "You mean I don't usually look slim and sexy?"

"Not really." Meg busted out into a fit of laughter. "You know I didn't mean that. I think the bubbly has gone to my head already."

"You are too funny." Andi lifted the hem of the dress and stepped off the platform. "Just for that, you have to start working out with me."

All signs of laughter faded from Meg's face. "Please don't make me go to the gym. There are bubbly college kids named Tiffany and Crystal at the gym."

"Wrong decade. Their names are now Madison and Isabella."

"You know what I mean."

"We'll work out in my living room," Andi said as she stepped back into the dressing room.

"Tell me you don't have your mother's Jane Fonda workout video."

"No." She closed the curtain and then unzipped the dress. "My mother wore out that tape years ago."

"That's a relief!"

Andi smirked as she slipped the dress back on its hanger. "I bought a DVD boot camp made by a real marine."

"Oh, great!" Meg moaned. "Not that I couldn't use a good workout. I popped a button off my black slacks last week."

"This DVD guarantees to take two inches off our waistline." Andi carried the dress out of the cramped room and handed it back to the sales clerk.

"Here." Meg lifted the glass waiting for her on the table. "I guess this is the last of our celebratory drinks."

Andi took a sip, enjoying the way it slid down her throat. "Don't look so depressed. I was teasing about the workout. I'm not changing anything about me for this wedding. I plan to keep it small, and everyone invited already knows I carry an extra inch here, there, and everywhere."

"And those of us who love you appreciate your down to earth attitude." Meg held her glass high.

They clinked glasses and then downed the rest of the bubbly liquid.

As they made their way to Andi's car, she spotted some of The Water Guppies parked in front of the bank at the end of the strip mall. Lorraine walked toward the building while Martha and Irene remained in Lorraine's white, luxury sedan. "Why is Lorraine carrying a knitting bag into a bank?"

"Good question," Meg said. "It looks like she's carrying something the size of a baby blanket inside of the bag."

"That, or a dozen skeins of yarn." Andi climbed into the driver's side of her car.

Meg rushed to open the passenger door and join her. "Should we head over there?"

"No. I have the feeling they're up to something." Andi flipped the power buttons to roll down their windows. "Let's wait here for her to return, and then we can follow them."

"Oh, goodie! A stakeout!"

"You crack me up." Andi retrieved a bag of chips from the console between them. "I always keep my car stocked for such an occasion."

"Drinks?"

"Cooler on the back seat."

Meg retrieved two diet sodas. "I'm impressed."

"I've learned a lot from my sister, aside from the usual self-defense moves."

They spent the next ten minutes eating, drinking, and waiting. Soon, Lorraine walked out of the bank with the flat bag she had folded and now carried with one hand.

Meg reached for another chip. "Do you think she delivered something she made to someone inside the bank?"

"It's a possibility." Andi turned her car's engine over as she watched Lorraine slide into the driver's seat of her sedan.

Meg buckled her seatbelt, while Andi drove out of the parking lot and turned right onto the busy street. She kept two cars between them to reduce the likelihood that any of The Water Guppies would spot them. When they neared the mall, Lorraine turned into the parking lot of another bank. Andi continued down the street until they reached an ice cream shop. She parked next to a tree, close enough for her to watch The Water Guppies.

This time Martha and Irene walked into the second bank with overstuffed bags made out of fabric patterns showing kittens playing with yarn. They looked like two older women joining a knitting circle.

Meg leaned closer to the window. "I bet they're putting something into their safety deposit boxes."

"All three of them?" Andi patted the steering wheel with both hands. "They could be hiding money."

"It's too bad we can't get close enough to know for sure." Meg took a sip of her soda and then placed the can back in the car's cup holder.

"We *can* see if they're here to see a teller or the safety deposit boxes. That would narrow down the possibilities." Andi pushed open her driver's side door. "If you'll follow them inside, I'll pay Lorraine a visit. She looks lonely, sitting in the car all by herself."

"If I remember right, she's the one most likely to talk." Meg jumped out and pushed her door shut. "I love playing spy!"

"Detective," Andi corrected.

"Detective." Meg weaved between cars as she headed toward the bank.

Andi snuck up behind the white sedan and pushed down on the trunk. The car bounced up and down on its tires, and Lorraine jerked around in her seat. Meg glanced in their direction and used that moment of distraction to rush inside the bank unnoticed.

"Lorraine!" Andi motioned for her to roll down the window, which she did. "Funny bumping into you here."

"Why?" Lorraine glanced toward the bank doors. Luckily, Meg had already made her way inside.

"Why, what?" Andi said.

"Why is it funny to bump into me in a bank parking lot?"

"I don't know. I guess it's a saying."

"I never heard it before," Lorraine said nervously. She

folded her hands in her lap and avoided looking directly at Andi. She blew out the breath she held when Martha and Irene exited the bank with folded knitting bags in their hands. "What are you doing here?" Lorraine asked.

"Meg needed to cash a check."

Lorraine's jaw dropped, and her eyes grew as wide as saucers. "Meg is in the bank?"

"Yep." Andi leaned closer to the car window. "I bet she ran into Irene and Martha—if that is who you came with."

As if on cue, Meg practically skipped out through the doors. Andi motioned for her to join them.

"Andi," Irene said when she reached the passenger's side. "It's so nice to see you again so soon."

"You, too. I guess everyone needed money today." Andi smiled at Martha and pointed to her folded knitting bag when she climbed into the back passenger seat. "Looks like you had a deposit."

"You're nosey, my dear," Martha said before closing the car door.

Andi grinned like a Cheshire cat. "I get paid to be nosey."

"Hi!" Meg bounced up beside Andi.

"We would love to chat, but we need to make a trip to the fabric store," Lorraine said.

"What a coincidence!" Meg pulled open the driver's side back door. "I was just telling Andi about the button I lost on my favorite pair of slacks." She climbed inside before they could object. "It's so nice of you to take me with you."

"But..." Lorraine stammered.

Andi walked away as fast as her legs would carry her. *I wish Meg had the spycam bird with her right now.*

****

Andi stopped by the grocery store before heading home. All the while, she kept thinking about Meg, wondering if she was able to get any of The Water Guppies to tell her what they were doing at the bank.

When she turned onto the busy street that led to

72

Euphoria Lane Condominiums, she spotted Lorraine's white sedan up ahead. *They must have left the fabric store at about the same time I left the grocery store.*

Movement in the sky caught Andi's attention. She leaned over her steering wheel, trying to get a good look at the object through her car window. It was black and looked like a spider. "A drone? What fool is flying a drone so close to the street?"

In her line of vision, she could see Lorraine pull into the middle of the intersection to make a left-hand turn. The Water Guppy accelerated, and the drone dived toward the driver's side of the window, forcing her to turn wide. At the last possible second, the drone swerved and then flew away. Lorraine lost control of the car and drove head-on into a brick wall.

"No!" Andi pressed down hard on the gas pedal until she reached the intersection.

Several other cars pulled over to the side. A middle-aged woman wearing a black pantsuit stood beside her car, speaking into her cell phone—hopefully to a 9-1-1 operator. An internet repairman jumped out of his van and ran toward the accident. Andi made the turn and drove the short distance to a residential street where she parked in front of the home of a couple who were already running out their front door, presumably to discover who had hit their backyard wall.

Andi pushed open her car door and ran as fast as she could back to the corner. If anything happened to Meg because of her investigation, she would never forgive herself. *What was she thinking, getting in the car with those criminals? If they are criminals. What am I thinking? The accident isn't their fault.*

By the time she reached the car, two men were assisting The Water Guppies.

Martha stood next to a young pizza delivery driver, assuring him she was fine. "I think I'm in shock. Other than that, I only have a scrape on my arm."

The homeowners examined the damage to their wall, including the bricks that had fallen on top of the car's hood.

The internet repairman spoke to Lorraine, who remained in the driver's seat with her hand lifted to her bloody forehead. "Here's a clean rag from my truck. Keep it pressed against the wound to stop the bleeding."

Andi tugged open the back door and found Meg quietly sitting in her seat, appearing both pale and dazed.

"Are you okay?" Andi searched for blood but didn't find any.

"I think so." Meg blinked rapidly. "I hit my head against the side of the car before the seatbelt pulled me tight." She lifted her hand to her ear. "Do I have a bruise?"

Andi ran her finger over the side of her friend's head. "You have a goose egg." She glanced into the front seat. "Irene, are you okay?"

"I think I have a concussion." Irene held her head with both hands. "I hurt so bad, and I feel dizzy."

"I'll call nine-one-one just in case no one else did." Andi reached for the phone she kept in her pocket.

The pizza guy, who had been helping Martha, leaned into the car. "I already called. Help will be here any minute." He glanced over at Lorraine in the front seat. "I still can't believe a drone attacked your car!"

I didn't imagine the drone! "Did you see who was controlling it?"

He removed his company hat and ran his hand through his hair. "If the owner was close, he was well hidden."

A whimper escaped from Lorraine's lips. "When I saw that thing in the sky, I thought it was falling on us."

Meg leaned close to Andi and whispered, "Lorraine escaped death for a second time. You know what they say..."

Andi couldn't speak the words out loud. *The third time's a charm.*

SIX

Andi drowned in her feelings of guilt as she gazed down at Meg, resting in her hospital bed. Her friend's angelic heart-shaped face looked so pale. *I should have demanded that she get out of Lorraine's car. She had no business trying to pump The Water Guppies for information.*

The smell of alcohol and the stark white surroundings were a constant reminder that someone could have died. Hours had ticked by slowly since Lorraine hit the wall with her car, and during that time, the doctors subjected Meg to one test after another. The monitor showed her heart rate, blood pressure, and temperature. Every time it beeped, Andi almost jumped out of her skin. She gingerly placed her hand on her friend's arm and studied her cloudy, blue eyes. "It won't hurt you to spend one night here."

"I feel foolish." Meg lifted the covers over her depressingly ugly hospital gown. "I'm perfectly fine."

"You have a concussion, and it must be serious if they want to keep an eye on you." Andi handed her a cup of ice chips.

"Are they keeping Irene overnight?" They had already discussed the fact that The Water Guppy had suffered a concussion as well.

Andi nodded. "She's miserable. She has a bruised face

and swollen lips. Everything above her neck is sore."

Meg sighed. "I feel so bad for her."

"There you are." Mack surprised everyone when he appeared inside the door frame, holding a bouquet of pink roses. "I heard about the accident and came right over." He took another step forward and then hesitated. "I hope you don't mind. I wanted to make sure you're all right."

Meg blushed. "That was nice of you."

An expression of relief flickered over his face as he walked to the opposite side of the bed. He took Meg's hand in his. "I heard something about a drone. What happened?"

"Probably exactly what you heard." Meg glanced down at their joined hands and blushed again. "I was coming back from a fabric store with some of The Water Guppies when a drone attacked us."

"That's not something you hear every day." His voice took on a softer tone when he asked, "Why would anyone target you?"

Meg eyed Andi for help in answering his question.

"Who said anything about targeting anyone?" Andi asked. "Some kid was probably messing around with a drone when his parents weren't home." She didn't believe that for a second, but she wasn't going to give away her true thoughts. Mack was still basically a stranger. A stranger who sometimes left her wondering if he had secrets of his own.

"You're probably right." He squeezed Meg's hand and smiled down at her.

Andi noticed the way she looked up at him like a schoolgirl, and a twinge of guilt ate at her for thinking ill of him. Then the nurse entered the room, making it feel crowded. "I'm going to find Luke," Andi said. "I'll be right back."

Out in the hall, she checked her phone and discovered her fiancé had taken Meg's son to the cafeteria for dinner. When she glanced up, she spotted Martha, Lorraine, and Roxie coming her way. She steered them away from the busy nursing staff and down a hall toward an empty sitting room furnished with half a dozen cushioned chairs and a small coffee table. A hand sanitizer hung on the wall, and a water cooler stood in the corner.

"How is she doing?" Martha still looked haggard despite going home to shower and change into comfortable clothes before coming to the hospital.

"She'll be fine." Andi sat in one of the chairs and waited for everyone else to join her before she continued. "This is getting serious, ladies."

Martha and Lorraine shared conspiratorial glances.

"Enough!" Roxie waggled her finger at her friends. "Tell Andi what she needs to know before someone else gets killed."

Martha leaned closer and whispered, "We've been investing money in the stock market."

"And..." Andi waited for the rest of the story.

"We've had some help," Lorraine said.

"Help?" Roxie arched a brow. "What kind of help?"

Andi studied Roxie's expression for any sign of deceit. "You *really* didn't know about this?"

"I told you I didn't know! I wish I had," she said, glaring at her friends. "I could have used some extra money, too." She framed her heavily made-up face with her hands. "Beauty like this doesn't come cheap."

Andi resisted the urge to roll her eyes and, instead, turned back to Lorraine. "Explain *help*."

Lorraine looked as guilty as a kid caught with her hand in a cookie jar. "My cousin Quin—the man in the picture from your security footage you asked about—is a security guard at a brokerage company. He overheard some things no one else was meant to hear—like information about businesses that would give an investor an upper hand in the stock market."

Roxie broke out in a fit of laughter. "You're committing insider trading? If that doesn't beat all. I thought you were smuggling human placenta or some other anti-aging serum over the border."

"Shh!" Martha scolded. "Don't shout it to the whole hospital. This is why we didn't tell you in the first place. You can't keep a secret!"

Roxie appeared to think over her accusation and then

shrugged. "Guilty as charged. At least gossiping isn't going to land me in prison."

Lorraine moaned. "I'm too old to go to prison. I can't be a big, hairy woman's girlfriend. I shave under my arms. I give to charities. I'm a good girl."

Roxie laughed harder. "Sorry, but this is too funny. Imagine the three of you committing felonies. It's like Santa's elves committing armed robbery."

"Roxie, control yourself." Andi switched chairs to sit next to Lorraine. "I'll do what I can to keep you out of prison, but I need to know what is going on. *Who* is trying to kill you?"

"I don't know." Lorraine searched her purse for a business card. "Here. This is my cousin's taxidermy card. It's a side business he runs out of his garage. You should talk to him."

Andi knew the general location of the address listed on the card. Quin Reed lived in an older neighborhood about ten minutes away.

Lorraine continued. "My cousin planted a listening device in the office of the man who had the information about these businesses. Quin thinks the guy found the bug hidden under his desk."

Roxie broke into another fit of laughter. "He *overheard* something, huh?"

Lorraine narrowed her eyes and waved her off. "My cousin *did* overhear him—at first." She directed her next statement to Andi. "About a week ago, someone broke into Quin's house but didn't take anything. Then he suspected a car might be following him. The driver took off before he could write down the license plate. Quin also told me he was afraid he might have led this guy over to my condo before he realized he had a tail."

Andi gestured with the card. "I'm going to go talk to your cousin today. I need to know who this other guy is before he gets another chance to attack."

"I'm going with you." Roxie jumped to her feet.

"Me, too," Lorraine said. "You have to take me. My cousin won't speak to you unless I'm there."

They all turned to Martha. "I...I'm going to stay here.

After I check on Meg, I'll keep an eye on Irene. If she's left alone, the bad guy could make a move on her."

Lorraine widened her eyes in fear.

Andi patted Martha's shoulder. She hated to admit the killer might try to finish the job right here in the hospital, but it was a possibility they needed to address. She lifted her phone to her ear. "I'll ask Luke and Meg's son to keep an eye on all of you while we're gone."

****

Meg looked up into Mack's dazzling blue eyes, wondering why a handsome man like him would take the time to visit her in the hospital. He had to have better things to do.

He flashed a warm smile. "I'm glad you're okay. I was worried."

He released her hand to set the vase down on the table, and she missed his touch.

"There was no need to worry. I'm a tough old bird."

"You may be tough, but you're nowhere near being old." He smiled and then pulled a chair closer to the bed. "I know you're good friends with Andi, so I was wondering why you were with The Water Guppies when the accident occurred. Andi wasn't with you."

She shrugged, trying to appear nonchalant. She wasn't about to tell him she was playing detective. "They were going to a fabric store, and I needed a button. Andi had other things to do. Nothing strange about that."

"You know condo complexes are like small towns. The rumor mill runs overtime, and they tend to embellish the truth." He rubbed his square jaw with the pad of his thumb. "I *hope* they are embellishing the truth."

She furrowed her brow. "Why? What are they saying?"

He leaned closer and lowered his voice. "They're saying whoever killed Betsy is trying to kill Lorraine."

"Really? They're saying that, huh?"

"They are." He seemed to study her response. "Do you think someone is trying to kill Lorraine?"

"I don't know why anyone would want to kill a little

old lady who looks like Mrs. Claus." *That is true,* Meg thought. *I don't know why someone is trying to kill her. She hasn't told me.*

"What happened today?"

"The accident?"

"Was it an accident?"

"Well, Lorraine didn't mean to drive into a backyard wall."

"Meg, what caused her to drive into the wall?"

"A drone almost hit us."

"Was it flying over you or *at* you?"

She hesitated, unable to meet his gaze.

"Meg...I care about you. Please, tell me what is going on here."

"I don't know." She finally glanced up into his worried eyes. "I believe someone is trying to kill her, but I don't know why. She's a sweet lady."

He squeezed her hand. "You should stay away from her. You could have died today."

She pulled back her hand and glared at him. "Would you desert your friends if they were in danger?"

He straightened his spine. "No, of course not."

"Then don't ask me to."

****

Andi turned into the older residential neighborhood. Large oil stains marred most of the concrete driveways, while yards proved to be neglected by large patches of dirt or weeds.

"My cousin still isn't answering his phone," Lorraine said from the back seat.

"Does he take your calls right away?" Andi checked the numbers printed on the curb to find the one that matched the business card she held in her hand.

"If he isn't on a date," Lorraine said.

Roxie, who rode shotgun, said, "He isn't going to answer the door if he got lucky after a lunch date. You know what I mean?"

"Yes, we know what you mean." Andi slowed as they

neared the address.

"He'll answer the door if I yell loud enough." Lorraine pointed to a blue house with an older model pickup truck parked in front of a closed one-car garage. The yard, covered with yellowing grass, appeared to have been abandoned long ago. "That's his house! He has to be home. He doesn't go anywhere without his truck."

Andi parked along the curb, and the three women walked over the flagstone steps toward the porch. Once they reached the door with peeling white paint, Lorraine knocked several times. No one answered.

Roxie tried the knob, and just like at Lorraine's condo, it turned and opened.

Andi's pulse skipped a beat.

Lorraine entered first. "Quin! It's me!"

Andi had a terrible feeling in her gut. She scanned the living room, sparsely decorated with a dark couch, coffee table, and flatscreen television. The only picture on the wall was of rodeo clowns running from a bull—*interesting taste in art.*

They paused briefly to study the kitchen. A full bowl of soggy cereal had been left behind on a wooden table crowded with unopened mail. Andi didn't know if it was the sink full of dirty dishes or the overflowing trash can emitting a sour smell.

She remembered he was a taxidermist and walked over the laminated floor to the garage door. Nothing could have prepared her for what she saw when she flipped on the light. At least twenty stuffed birds hung from the ceiling. Their open beaks and vise-like claws created the image of an impending attack like the ones Hitchcock created in his famous movie, *The Birds.* Her breath caught in her throat.

After she recovered from her initial shock, she noticed the maze of wooden picnic tables and benches filling most of the garage. Tools, supplies, and stuffed animals covered most of the flat surfaces. In a corner, next to a pile of flat packing boxes, a stiff coyote with black marble eyes guarded its territory. Dirt scattered around its paws gave the scene a realistic, desert appearance.

Roxie poked her head into the garage. "Don't make this guy mad. He's good at what he does. If he knocks you out and stuffs you, we won't know you're dead."

"Funny." Andi flipped off the light and secured the eerie scene behind the closed door.

When they failed to find Quin in the laundry room, they started down the hall. He wasn't in the bathroom or spare room, either.

Lorraine walked heavily toward the last unsearched area in the house, which had to be the master bedroom. The closed door loomed ahead. "He must be taking a nap."

"Or..." Roxie grinned.

"It's too quiet in there for anyone to be having afternoon delight," Lorraine said, referring to an old song lyric. She tapped on the door. "Quin, it's your cousin Lorraine." No answer. She knocked louder. "Quin!"

Roxie turned the knob and then pushed the door open. Her expression morphed from confusion to fear.

Andi shifted and spotted the bloody arm on the floor. The unmade bed hid the rest of the body from view.

Lorraine gasped, and Andi grabbed her arm before she could rush forward.

Roxie was the only one who dared to enter the room. She walked around the navy-blue comforter that had fallen off the king-sized bed and then stood over the body and grimaced. "Keep her out. This is ugly."

Lorraine broke free of Andi's hold and ran inside like a frantic child. She fell to the beige carpet next to her dead cousin. "Quin," she cried. "No! Not Quin!"

Andi bent and held onto Lorraine's shoulders, wishing she could do more. The aroma of sweaty socks overpowered any smell the body might have given off. Quin had died from an apparent gunshot wound to the chest. A revolver and pillow—which looked like it had been used to stifle the sound—had fallen near this body.

She remembered the cereal left on the kitchen table. It wasn't that old.

He must have died within the past couple of hours.

Roxie gestured with her head toward the oak dresser, and Andi stepped closer until she spotted what appeared to be a suicide note. "To my friends and family," she read aloud. "I am sorry I don't have the courage to live. They fired me at work, and I'm too old to find a new job. I refuse to become a burden on my family. I love you all."

Lorraine suddenly stopped crying and lifted her head to look at Andi. "Why would he care if he lost his job? He made as much money as I did on those investments. He bought a house in the Cayman Islands and was planning to move there next month. He had enough money to live quite comfortably—even if he reached the ripe old age of a hundred and fifty."

Andi pictured the stack of packing boxes in the garage. "Don't touch anything!" She lifted her hands in a halt position and slowly stepped away from the dresser. "The police will need to dust for fingerprints."

"You're right," Roxie said. "No one uses a pillow to muffle a gunshot when they commit suicide."

Andi wrapped her arm around the distraught woman and helped her up off the ground. "We need to find out who your cousin got his insider information from before—"

"He kills me," Lorraine whispered.

****

The next morning, Andi stood in front of the receptionist's desk, waiting for the twenty-something woman at Lincoln and Martin Investments to finish directing a call. The Scottsdale firm gleamed with polished glass, stone, and metal.

Andi watched Roxie play with the leaves of a fake floor plant. No one could accuse that Water Guppy of being patient. Meanwhile, Lorraine stood near the hall to the offices. With a little luck, she might overhear something useful.

The receptionist, who wore a black shift dress with a white collar, pushed a button on her phone system and then smiled up at them. "Can I help you?"

She handed her one of her business cards. "I'm Detective Andi Stevenson."

"I hired her," Roxie said.

Lorraine stepped over to the desk. "Me, too." She wiped away a tear. "My cousin is...*was* Quin Reed."

"*Was?*" The woman's smile faded. Her phone rang, and she pushed another button, terminating the incoming call.

"He died today." Lorraine patted her puffy, blood-shot eyes with a tissue.

"Did he have a locker or desk?" Andi asked. "We're here for his belongings."

"I'm so sorry for your loss." She pushed a stray strand of long, straight blonde hair behind her ear. "Mr. Reed was a nice man." The phone rang again, and this time the woman quickly dispatched the call to one of the brokers. "Did he tell you he left anything behind?"

Roxie blew out a big, noisy breath and slapped the desk. "Of course not. He's dead."

"I'm sorry. I didn't mean..."

"Nothing to be sorry about, dear," Lorraine said in her grandmotherly tone.

"What I meant to say is I saw Mr. Reed leave with a box on his last day." The girl glanced at Roxie as if expecting to be verbally rebuked again.

Andi rubbed her forehead. *This isn't getting us anywhere.* "When was his last day?"

"Two days ago." The receptionist glanced down sheepishly. "May I ask how he passed away?"

"Gunshot to the heart," Roxie said abruptly. "Now, maybe you can tell us why your firm fired him."

The woman gasped. "I'm sorry. I can't help you. I wish I could."

"Who *can* help us?" Andi asked, aiming for polite but missing the mark. Her patience was running as thin as Roxie's. They didn't have time to waste.

"Our office manager," the woman said, regaining control of her professional demeanor. "She'll be back tomorrow."

"Please give her my card." Andi escorted Lorraine to the main entrance. She was about to tug on the metal handle when Mack appeared on the other side of the glass doors. His gaze met Andi's, and he blinked repeatedly.

Once he recovered from his surprise, he pulled open the door and held it for them. "Funny meeting you here."

"I'm surprised you're not back at the hospital with Meg," Roxie said as she followed the others into the breezeway and away from the glass doors.

"I was." He rubbed his jaw. "She was fine when I left her with Luke and her son an hour ago. The doctor is going to release her today."

"I'll need to head over there," Andi said. "She might need a ride."

"Her son has it taken care of." Mack sounded apologetic. "He seems like a responsible young man."

"He is," Andi said. She tilted her head and met his gaze. "It's odd bumping into you so far from the condos. Do you invest with Lincoln and Martin?"

"Me? Oh, no." He glanced around at the surrounding businesses and then pointed to the nearby travel agency with a colorful, cardboard flamingo and pink neon OPEN sign in the window. "I'm headed over there. I was thinking of going on a cruise. I never had time to travel when I owned my dental practice. I always had to worry about paying our overhead."

Andi nodded, even though she didn't believe he drove forty minutes from their complex to book a cruise. *His whole body was facing the door to the investment company, and he was about to open the door when he spotted us.* "That reminds me of another question I had."

"Oh?" He eyed her speculatively.

"Why won't you answer anyone's dental questions? You were a dentist, weren't you?"

Roxie narrowed her eyes at him. "Did you have a traumatic experience you don't want to remember?"

Mack chuckled. "No. I don't want to give anyone advice contrary to their dentist's instructions. Bacteria in the gums can lead to serious illnesses, and I no longer carry professional insurance."

"That makes sense." Roxie threw up her hands and retreated.

"Yes, it does," Andi admitted. "We should get going. Have fun planning your cruise."

He lifted his finger and then pointed to the travel agency. "Right, well, I'll see you all later."

Andi watched him walk away. Once he disappeared behind the double doors, she waved for the others to follow her to a bench in front of a weight-loss establishment, located next door to the investment firm. They sat side-by-side, and she turned to Roxie. "Did you bring the listening device like I asked?"

"Of course. I'm going to keep it close until this investigation is over."

They had all agreed that Roxie should hold onto the device since it was probably illegal to use, and the unconventional woman didn't mind skirting the law. Just when Andi was beginning to wonder whether or not she had brought it with her, Roxie reached behind the top of her zebra-print jumpsuit and inside her bra.

"No..." Andi whined. "You hid it there—again!"

"No better hiding place." Roxie put one bud in her ear and held out the other for Andi. "Do you want to listen or not?"

Andi pulled the bottom hem of her shirt out far enough to catch the bud. "Drop it in here."

"Really?!" Roxie rolled her eyes and then flicked it off her bony fingers. "You're a wimp."

"True." Andi wiped the earbud with her shirttail and then placed it in her ear, waiting to hear any conversations inside the nearby businesses. She motioned for Roxie to turn it on. It would be easy to differentiate from people wanting to invest their money wisely from people wanting to shed unwanted pounds.

"What are we listening for?" Roxie asked.

"Anything about Quin," Lorraine said. "If someone just told you an employee—who just got fired—died from a gunshot, you would be gossiping." Her pained expression echoed the emotion in her voice.

Andi lifted her finger. "I hear something."

"What?" Lorraine asked.

"Shh." Roxie tapped the earbud. "I can't hear."

"He's my cousin! I should get to listen!"

Roxie sighed and then held the bud out. "It's been in

my bra *and* my ear."

"Never mind." Lorraine backed away.

"That's what I thought." Roxie placed it back in her ear. At least she didn't smirk.

"I'll share," Andi said. She held the earbud between them so they could both hear, and then tried to focus on the conversation between the receptionist and another employee.

"Are you sure he's dead?" a woman with a high-pitched voice asked.

"That's what they said." The voice belonged to the receptionist. "They wanted his belongings. I got the impression that they didn't know HR fired him for stealing from Brad."

"Would you tell your relatives you stole money out of someone's desk?"

"Probably not," the receptionist said.

Lorraine's eyes grew wide. Andi could tell she was dying to tell them something.

"Wait till Brad comes back from Wyoming and discovers Quin is dead," the woman with the high-pitched voice said.

"About that," the receptionist said. "Why do you think Quin broke into Brad's office in the first place? Why not the CEO's office?"

"Maybe he thought Brad was doing something illegal or immoral and wanted blackmail material. I'm only guessing," the other woman said.

"I wouldn't be surprised to learn Brad is up to no good," the receptionist said. "Do you think the higher-ups will look into it?"

"No. They would consider it inviting trouble."

"True."

When it became apparent that the women had concluded their gossiping, Andi took the bud out of her ear. It took less than a minute on her smartphone to find Brad's last name on the firm's website.

Lorraine motioned for them to follow her further away from Lincoln and Martin Investments. "My cousin bugged the office of the guy who was doing insider trading. He had overheard the conversation that started all of this by accident when they were both out of the office. We couldn't make any other investments unless we knew what this Brad guy knew, so Quin bugged his office. When he caught someone following him, he got scared and snuck back into the guy's office to remove the bug. Only it wasn't there. Brad must have claimed he caught him stealing money from his desk to get rid of him."

Andi showed the list of Lincoln and Martin's investment brokers on her phone to Roxie and Lorraine. There was only one Brad. "Keep an eye out for this guy. I think he's our killer."

SEVEN

Andi needed to come up with a game plan to catch the killer, but first, she needed to hide Lorraine in a safe place.

"No need to worry," Lorraine's sweet, grandmotherly voice drifted to the front seat of the car. "I'm staying with Roxie. No one will get by her."

I hope no one tries.

"The Water Guppies are staying with me until this is over." Roxie gave a half shrug. "Well, the ones that aren't partying in the Caribbean. And since Lorraine never included them in these shenanigans, there's no need to worry about them."

"Irene and Martha are waiting for us at Roxie's," Lorraine said. "It will be like a slumber party!" Although she tried to sound enthusiastic, her tone missed the mark. Andi appreciated the effort just the same.

"That's probably a good idea. Safety in numbers." Andi drove on to Roxie's condo. She dropped them off with a wave and a smile she hoped would help calm Lorraine, and then checked her text messages. *Nothing yet.*

Meg had promised to notify her once Chad brought her home.

Andi pulled into her garage and turned off the ignition. She drew in a deep breath and sat in the silence within her car. *How am I going to catch a killer and protect these grandmas?*

Once she could no longer justify sitting alone in her car, she climbed out and spotted Poppy, their new neighbor and veterinary student, standing in the small patch of grass the complex considered a front yard. *I hope this is a social call. I don't need another HOA complaint.*

Poppy waved. "I just came from the clubhouse. There's a sign that says the baking lesson was canceled for tonight."

Andi pushed her car door shut and walked over to the veterinary student, who had seemed excited about continuing with the baking classes. "I'm sorry about the cancellation. A lot is going on right now. We'll continue with the classes soon. I promise."

Her expression turned solemn. "I heard about the car accident. Is everyone all right?"

"Irene and Meg have concussions, but the doctors believe they will both be fine—as long as they don't go hitting their heads again anytime soon." Andi smiled. "It's nice of you to be concerned."

"The neighbors around here have been good to me. I hated to hear the news." Poppy shook her head and frowned. "I can't believe someone would cause a car accident with a drone. Those things need to be banned!"

"I couldn't believe it either, and I saw the whole thing."

"Really? Did you see who was controlling the drone?"

"No. I wish I had. I would say someone should go to jail, but I have a feeling it might have been a kid." *Not really, but I'm not going to feed the rumor mill.*

Poppy nodded. "You're probably right." She crossed her hands over her chest. "I also heard about Lorraine's cousin. How is she doing?"

"That rumor mill doesn't miss anything, does it?"

Poppy cringed. "I guess not. It's a small community, and it seems like there are a lot of people who know each other."

"That's true. Lorraine's shaken, but I'm sure she'll be okay. She has good friends who are sticking close to help her through the worst of it."

"That's good. I know how hard it is to recover from a

loved one's suicide."

Suicide? That's interesting. The rumor mill must have heard about the suicide note and locked onto that detail. "I'm sorry to hear you lost someone as well."

Poppy turned at the sound of Luke driving up to the curb.

"Have you met my fiancé?" Andi asked.

Poppy's smile lit up her face. "I haven't had the pleasure. Congratulations! The last I heard he was your boyfriend. The engagement must be recent." She glanced down at her left hand. "What a beautiful ring!"

"He has great taste in jewelry." Andi made the introductions, and after Poppy left, Luke led her inside.

"How are you doing?" He pulled her in for a much-needed hug.

She rested her head against his chest and took in the aroma of his spicy cologne. "Better now. Poor Lorraine. She kept a brave front during our visit to the investment company, but I know it must have been difficult. None of us will forget finding her cousin's body. It was horrible."

"I'm glad you were there for her." He kissed her tenderly and then made himself at home in her kitchen.

She booted up her laptop at the dining room table. "I'm searching for this Brad guy who got Lorraine's cousin fired," she said, loud enough for him to hear. "Brad's name was on the company website, but not his picture."

"Why did the cousin get fired?"

"We think Brad found the bug Quin—that's her cousin—had planted in his office. Brad claimed he caught Quin breaking into his office and stealing money from his desk."

"The Water Guppies admitted to you that they are guilty of insider trading thanks to Lorraine's cousin, correct?"

"Correct. Brad is the source of the information they used to invest." She scanned through the list of documents on her screen after entering his name into the search engine."

"Quin's bug most likely recorded the conversations Brad had in his office," Luke said loud enough for her to hear from the kitchen. "Brad must have felt he had no choice; he had to get rid of Quin."

"It gets worse," Andi said. "Lorraine thinks Brad followed her cousin to her place, and that is why he is trying to kill her."

"That makes sense." Luke carried in two plates containing tuna sandwiches and chips. "He thinks she knows too much. If he saw Betsy and Lorraine together, he might have rightly guessed that Betsy knew too much as well. He might have even figured out that they were both investing with his information."

"Betsy might have been targeted first because she was flaunting her wealth. She wore pricey clothes and drove a fancy car." Andi selected the largest chip on her plate. "Big purchases, especially in cash, might trigger an audit. He couldn't risk her talking if she got caught."

"I'm glad The Water Guppies are sticking together," Luke said. "They're safer if they are keeping their eyes open as a group. Unless someone blows up their condo."

"Bite your tongue!"

"I'm just saying they need to be on the lookout for every possibility. I'll check Roxie's smoke detectors after lunch."

"Here!" Andi turned her laptop to face Luke. "This is Brad." The picture showed a clean-cut, thirty-something professional. "He looks familiar, but I can't place him."

"I know what you mean. You should go over the security footage from the bird camera across from the gate. You might spot him coming onto the property. That would help prove he's the killer." Luke lifted half of her sandwich to her mouth. "Eat."

She grinned and bit off one end. "Hmm. Thank you." After swallowing, she asked, "Did you find anything about our new neighbor, Mack?"

He shook his head and swallowed. "Nothing. The owner doesn't know much about him, except for glowing reports from his references."

She entered Mack's name, and nothing came up. She checked in images. Still nothing. "That's interesting." This time she added *dentist* to his name. Again, nothing. "You would think a dentist's name would come up in a search."

"Mack could be his middle name or even a nickname."

"True. The next time you run into him, would you ask a few questions to see what you can uncover?"

"Of course." He leaned in for another kiss. "Do you want his name, rank, and serial number?"

She smiled. "All of the above." She leaned back from the laptop. "I forgot to tell you that he showed up at Lincoln and Martin Investments where Quin worked. When he spotted us, he acted like he was there to visit a travel agency. My gut says this guy isn't who he says he is."

"Trust your gut," Luke said. "It's usually right."

****

Andi drove to the hospital after Meg told her the doctor hadn't released her yet. Pent-up tension eased from her shoulders when she discovered her friend looked more like herself. Meg had regained most of the color in her face and appeared eager to escape what she referred to as the institution of boredom. She loved being a nurse, not a patient.

"What's the hold-up?" Andi read the monitor, not sure what any of the numbers stood for or meant.

"My doctor had an emergency to attend to this morning." Meg fluffed her pillow and then dropped back onto the bed. "He should be starting his rounds soon."

"Where's Chad?"

"I told him to go to work. There was no need for him to stick around here if you were on your way. He was going nuts sitting around here waiting and waiting."

"He has less patience than you do."

"That's saying a lot." She folded the top of her blanket down and then adjusted her gown. "How is Lorraine doing? She must be a mess after finding her cousin's body."

Andi cringed at the memory. Finding Quin like that would haunt her dreams for the rest of her life. "Lorraine is stronger than we thought. And I think it did her good to go to the investment firm. She needed to help find her cousin's murderer." Andi caught Meg up on their trip to Lincoln and Martin Investments.

"That's a big clue." Meg reached for her cup of water. "I'm confused about Mack, though.

"Did I hear my name?" Mack poked his head inside the doorframe.

Roxie bumped into him as she barged in before anyone could answer. She wore a pink-and-purple striped jumpsuit and teal-colored stilettos. Her heels almost matched her mint-green, beehive hairstyle. "Look who I ran into when I checked on Irene."

He combed his hair back into place with his fingers and then followed her to Meg's bedside.

"I was just telling Meg that we ran into Mack this morning," Andi said. "You seem to be everywhere." *Why?*

"I wanted to make sure Irene had a ride home." Mack lifted Meg's hand off the bed and held it within both of his. "You're looking a lot better. Not that you weren't beautiful the last time I saw you."

A wave of red flooded Meg's face. "I am feeling better. How is Irene?"

"Ready for real food," Roxie said. "If that doctor doesn't release her soon, she's going to crawl out the window, and I'm going to help her. Hospitals give me the creeps. Can you imagine how many ghosts roam the halls?"

"Speaking of ghosts," Andi said. "Mack, have you had any strange occurrences yet? The neighbors swear your condo is haunted. The woman living next door to you claims to see flickering lights."

He smirked. "Flickering lights usually means you have an electrical short, not a haunting."

"True," Andi said. "Except for the fact your landlord hired two different electricians, one in January and one in May, and neither could find a problem with the wiring."

"I'm telling you, you should have a séance," Roxie said. "That would be a real hoot!"

He frowned. "But you don't like ghosts."

"But I love dressing up as a gypsy for séances." Roxie pretended to wave her hands over a crystal ball. "I see dead people."

Meg grinned. "A séance would be fun."

Mack rubbed the back of her hand. "It looks like I'm

outnumbered. When do you want to hold this shindig?"

Meg shrugged. "Tonight?"

He furrowed his brow. "But you're—"

"No buts," Roxie said, almost jumping for joy. She grabbed his arm and pulled him toward the door. "Let's go tell Irene the good news."

After he left the room, Andi turned back to her friend. "You really want to hold a séance tonight?"

Meg rubbed the hand he had been holding. "You want to find out who this guy is, don't you?"

Andi glanced down at her friend's troubled expression. "I think you need to know who the real Mack is more than I do."

****

Later that night, Andi and Luke sat in Meg's living room, revisiting their plans for the séance. Andi adjusted the orange throw pillow behind her on the sofa. The bright colors in the room matched her friend's usually bright and cheery personality. After she healed from her wounds, she would return to herself, provided Mack didn't break her heart. Andi wouldn't let that happen. She would discover who the real Mack is before Meg fell too hard.

"You need to be the one to pretend to see Betsy's ghost," Andi told her friend. "You're a much better actress than I am."

"True." Meg grabbed a canvas bag from the shelf in her coat closet. "No offense. You're a better detective."

"No offense taken. I'm the one who said it first." Andi pressed her mind for ideas. They needed to get Mack to tell them why he was at the investment firm. "What if we pretend Mrs. Owens' ghost is speaking through you?"

"That's good!" Luke said. "You can moan and wail."

Andi chuckled. "You could moan eerily and tell Roxie there are souls on the other side anxious for her arrival."

Meg chuckled. "We don't want her to run out of the room screaming," she said as she placed a vanilla-scented pillar candle and mirrored plate into a canvas bag.

Andi handed her the book of matches she'd brought

with her for the event. "The important part is pretending Mrs. Owens wants Mack to move out of her home because he is keeping secrets."

"Watch his body language," Luke said. "He may reveal more by how he reacts than by what he says." He stood and took the bag from Meg. "Anything else we need?"

"I don't think so," Meg said. "Roxie is bringing a tablecloth. That and the candle should do it."

"Let's go!" Andi waited outside with Luke while Meg locked her front door.

Highway traffic hummed in the distance as they walked the short distance to Mack's condo. Streetlamps and the decorative outdoor lights illuminated the way. A crisp breeze forced Andi to button up her sweater. The recent rains had chased away the remnants of summer and welcomed in winter.

They found Mack's door open, and heard The Water Guppies before they saw them in the dining room. Roxie and Martha each held one side of a purple tablecloth and lowered it over a rectangular oak table. Martha wore all black like a burglar. Andi wondered if the Guppy intended to wander around in the dark and move objects like a ghost. She hoped not. There was no way Martha would get away with such a plan. The thought made Andi second guess theirs as well.

Roxie wore an off-the-shoulder peasant top that revealed her knobby shoulders. A waist wrap partially covered her red and tan striped skirt in gypsy fashion, and black boots topped off the outfit that could end up being her Halloween costume.

"Looks like the right place." Luke shut the door behind him.

"Come on in," Mack said. "I've never attended a séance before. Should I put out the cheese and crackers now or later?"

"We just ate," Andi said.

Meg lifted her finger. "I can always—"

"Eat later," Andi finished for her with a wide-eyed look at her friend. Rule number two in the detective manual she would one day write would state: Never eat in the home of a murder suspect. Rule number one: Never go alone to the home of a murder suspect. She had made that mistake before.

"Oh..." Meg finally caught on. "I will be starving *later*."

Andi suspected Mack wouldn't be in a generous mood to offer anyone anything by the time the séance ended. She sat next to Irene at the far end of the table and tried not to stare at the bruises marring her face from the car accident. "How are you feeling? Are you sure you're up to this?"

Irene patted Andi's hand resting on the table. "I'm fine. Just a bit sore. I'd rather be here than home watching TV."

"I understand." Andi sent her a warm smile. "I wouldn't want to miss the drama of a séance, either." She turned to find Meg centering the mirrored plate and pillar candle on top of the table.

Roxie lifted a brown shopping bag onto a chair and began unpacking more candles. She placed a half-dozen cinnamon-scented votive candles around the mirrored plate. Next, she placed red taper candles in ceramic holders a foot in from each corner of the table.

Andi's jaw dropped when Roxie lined up and then lit sets of candles shaped like ghosts, turkeys, snowmen, and Santas on the granite kitchen pass-through. "Isn't that overkill?"

"Not at all." Roxie then showed off her pilgrim candles. "We need to set the mood. It will improve our chances of summoning the ghost."

Andi glanced at Meg, who shrugged her shoulders.

They turned to Irene, who lifted her hands in a halt position. "Don't look at me. I might be as pale as a ghost in my current condition, but that doesn't make me an expert on dead people."

"Of course not!" they said in unison and then exchanged sheepish looks.

Mack handed everyone a water bottle. "It might be a good idea to discuss how we want to run this...gathering."

"I assume we'll all sit around the table and hold hands," Luke added. "At least that's what I've seen in the movies."

"Since I've attended more seances than I can count," Roxie said, "I'll run the show. It will be important for all of you to remain silent once I begin to speak to the spirits."

Andi glanced at Meg. The unspoken message was to continue with their plan despite what Roxie wants. While everyone chose a seat at the table, Andi scanned Mack's living room. He owned a brown sofa, coffee table, and flat-screen television. She expected more from someone who had a professional life in Chicago. She began to wonder if there was a former Mrs. Mack Young, who now owned the vast majority of their belongings. There was so much about him that they didn't know.

Andi waved to get Mack's attention. "Where's your bathroom?"

"Down the hall and to your right." He didn't appear concerned about her wandering through his home. Andi took that as a good sign for Meg.

She slipped down the hall and into the room, which contained only bare necessities. He had a white shower curtain, one hand towel, a roll of toilet paper, and a bottle of liquid soap. Not a single floor mat covered the brown tile. The man was either a minimalist, only planned to rent for a short time, or lost his belongings during the trip to Arizona. She flipped on the ceiling fan to cover the noise created when she opened the medicine cabinet. Mack could be a nickname. If so, she'd find his given name printed on any prescription bottles he might have. A man his age was bound to be taking at least one prescription medication. She almost jumped for joy when she found a single bottle on the bottom shelf. She held her breath as she turned it around and read, "Mack Young." *What?! His real name cannot be Mack Young. I didn't find anything on the internet under that name.*

Inside of the cabinet beneath the sink, she found a package of toilet paper and two brown bath towels and two brown washcloths. *Why is everything brown? Is he colorblind? No. His clothes aren't all one color.*

She washed her hands and then stepped out into the hall. Her eyes locked on the closed bedroom door. *Do I dare?*

Martha suddenly stepped into her line of vision. "Roxie is looking for you. She's getting impatient."

Andi drew in a deep breath. "I'm ready."

After she walked back to the dining room, she found Luke grabbing a gray folding chair. He leaned it against the wall and added it to the six wooden chairs at the table since there were seven people in attendance.

"Where's Lorraine?" Andi asked, scooting closer to both the table and Luke. She glanced at Meg and then gestured with her head toward the seat directly across from her. Her friend caught the hint.

Martha frowned. "Lorraine is spending the evening with her cousin's mother and sisters."

"Oh." Andi felt a tug at her chest. "I feel so bad for them."

Irene patted her hand again. "The older you get, the more often you have to say goodbye to those you love. I wish I could say you get used to it, but you don't."

Before Andi could mull over death and the truth behind her statement, Mack flipped off the light switch and chose the chair beside Meg. The holiday character candles in the pass-through provided enough light for them all to make out their surroundings.

Roxie struck a match and used it to light a taper candle, which she used to light the other candles on the table. She saved the bigger one in the middle for last. "Quiet," she ordered. "I am ready to begin!"

Andi bit her lip. *I have to let her do it her way—until Meg is ready to take over.*

Roxie lifted her hands into the air and began humming, which sounded like a type of meditation. The shadows cast by the flickering candles danced across her thin, overly made-up face. "We are here to speak to the spirit of the house." More humming, followed by swaying.

"Do you need a crystal ball?" Martha asked, her loud voice slicing through the dark like a knife.

"Shh! No. Shh!" Then Roxie's humming grew more intense.

"Betsy?" Meg asked, which wasn't what they had rehearsed. The candles illuminated Meg's widening eyes. She leaned back, away from the table, and stared at a spot over Andi's right shoulder.

Andi leaned forward and whispered, "Are you *sure* it's not Mrs. Owens? It is *her* house."

"Shh!" Roxie ordered. "I'm in charge, and I don't see anyone!"

Andi felt the temperature of the room grow cold and rubbed her arms for warmth. *Did Mack turn on the air conditioner?*

She listened. *No.*

There has to be a reasonable explanation.

If there were any open windows, she would be able to hear the highway in the distance. She couldn't.

A huff of frigid wind blew on her cheek. She jumped and spun around. No visible person stood behind her. *What was that?!* Searching around her in the candle-lit room, she examined the dancing shadows for anything out of place but found nothing.

Luke squeezed her hand, reminding her he was there for her if she needed him.

Meg stared harder, and her face trembled with apparent fear. With Martha holding one hand and Mack holding the other, she was unable to point to anything.

Andi's body grew rigid. She knew something or someone was standing right behind her in the darkness. She could feel the presence hovering over her, and goosebumps traveled down her arms. "Who's there?"

"Betsy," Meg whispered.

"Don't you mean Mrs. Owens?" Andi said, wishing they could go back to the plan where Meg would pretend Mrs. Owens' ghost was speaking through her.

Meg shook her head. "It's Betsy. Betsy is here—in this room."

"Where?" Irene narrowed her eyes, trying to find the ghost. "I don't see her."

"I think I do," Martha said. "I see a dark shadow behind Luke. It kind of looks like Betsy."

"She's standing behind Andi," Meg said.

"I knew I could conjure a spirit!" Roxie bounced in her chair with excitement. "I knew it!"

"Betsy," Martha said. "Are you happy? Have you found peace?" Martha turned to Meg. "Does she look younger in heaven?"

"Of course she's happy." Roxie groaned. "Heaven doesn't have a homeowners' association."

"Betsy," Meg said softly. "Is your murderer in this room?"

Everyone froze in place as they looked from one person to the next, all wondering if they held hands with a murderer.

After what seemed like an eternity, Meg released a long breath. "She's gone."

"Don't leave us hanging!" Roxie shook her hands free, breaking the chain and jumping to her feet. "Is there a murderer in this room or not?"

Meg shook her head.

Roxie planted her hands on her hips defiantly. "What do you mean, no?!"

"No one here killed Betsy," she said softly.

Roxie's huff mirrored her expression of disappointment.

"That's a good thing, Roxie," Andi said, while her mind tried to make sense of what had happened. "Betsy confirmed that our friends are not murderers."

"Right." Roxie tried to look happy but failed. "Of course I don't want our friends to be murderers. I was only thinking about how dramatic it would have been if Meg pointed at someone and said, *She did it! She's the murderer!*"

"Or him." Luke glanced at Mack and added, "The murderer could be a man."

"True," Mack said. "But not this one!" He stood. "I think that's enough excitement for one evening." He blew out the center candle with a huff of breath, flipped on the lights, and then marched down the hall.

I knew he wouldn't be offering us snacks after the séance, but I didn't know Luke would be the one to anger him.

Martha blew out the remaining candles, while Lorraine poured the hot wax into a mason jar and twisted the lid closed. Together they rolled the candles up in an old navy-blue beach towel with frayed edges and then packed them into a bag. Andi and Luke helped Roxie fold her tablecloth. No one spoke for several minutes.

Irene finally broke the silence. She sidled up next to Meg, who stood to the side, holding her pillar candle and mirrored plate. "I didn't know you were a medium."

"I'm not," Meg said. "At least I wasn't." She held one hand up to the side of her head. "It must be the concussion. Hallucinations can happen after suffering a brain injury."

"What did Betsy look like?" Martha asked. "Did she say anything?"

Meg furrowed her brow. Her pained expression made Andi cringe just looking at her.

"She only shook her head," Meg said. "She was like a mist, only clearer. I could barely see through her."

Irene joined the conversation. "What was she wearing?"

Meg tilted her head to the side as if trying to recall. "It was an old-fashioned blue dress with pearl buttons and a lace collar."

Martha dropped into a chair and then turned to look at Roxie.

"What?" Andi asked. "You know something about that dress."

Roxie pressed the folded tablecloth to her chest, her expression unreadable. "Betsy is going to be buried in that dress."

Martha took Meg's hands and held them in her own. "You didn't have a hallucination. You see dead people."

The color faded from Meg's face, and her eyes rolled up into her head.

Andi caught her before she hit the ground.

EIGHT

The next morning Andi received a call from one of the neighbors. The cat-fighting duo was at it again. She snatched her keys off the kitchen counter and complained to the walls, "What is it going to take to get these girls to stop?!"

After locking up, she marched down the road that circled the complex until she reached Emma's driveway, where they were yelling in each other's faces. *How did they ever become friends? They are so different.* Nina wore the uniform of a movie theatre employee: black slacks and a red polo shirt with the theatre's logo sewn on with yellow thread. Emma wore the uniform of overprivileged youth: high-priced designer everything from head to toe. *Who would have ever guessed black leggings and a long sweater could cost as much as a plane ticket to Miami?*

"What now?" Andi didn't bother hiding her impatience. "I thought you both got restraining orders against each other."

"I did get one!" Emma planted her hands on her hips. "And she already broke it. She's so pathetic! She was peeping into my window last night while Dylan and I were sleeping."

"Liar!" Nina screeched. "And how would you know if anyone was outside your window if you were sleeping.

Huh? Tell me that, will you?"

Andi drew in a calming breath, and then coughed on the overwhelming comingling of citrus and gardenia scented perfumes. She took several steps backward and then turned to Emma. "Did you wake up and catch her?"

"You bet I woke up! I heard a noise outside and thought someone was trying to break in through my bedroom window."

"And?" Andi waved her hand for her to continue.

Emma narrowed her eyes at Nina. "I jumped out of bed in time to see her walking away."

Nina pushed her long, brunette hair away from her face and then pointed at Emma with dramatic flair. "You did not see *me* because I wasn't there. I spent the night with a friend!"

"You liar! I can prove you were spying!" Emma pursed her pink-painted lips.

"Cannot!"

"Can so!" Emma pulled her phone out of her burgundy-colored sweater pocket and swiped the images on her screen until she found what she was looking for. "See!" She held it up for Andi to view. "See the stinking liar!"

Andi squinted to view the small, dark screen. She could make out a bush, grass, some shadows, and the toes of a white tennis shoe. "Yes, there was someone outside your window, but I can't tell if it's a man or a woman."

Nina snatched the phone and peered into the picture. "I wouldn't be caught dead in those shoes!"

"That can be arranged—if you insist," Emma said with a menacing glare.

"Enough!" Andi grabbed the phone and handed it back to Emma. "Are you trying to get arrested?"

"That can be arranged." Nina glared back.

There has to be a way to get through to these girls. "I heard that you two were good friends, once upon a time, before Dylan swapped one of you out for the other."

Emma crossed her hands over her chest. "What's that got to do with anything?"

Nina narrowed her eyes. "I'm just glad I discovered what a back-stabber she is before I wasted another minute on our so-called friendship."

Andi drew in a calming breath. "My point is any guy willing to break up a friendship to date both women probably doesn't care about anyone other than himself. I could be wrong, but I doubt it. My fiancé is a good man, and he would never come between best friends."

Nina smirked. "Dylan is a jerk, and he'll drop you, too," she told Emma. "You'll see."

Emma rolled her eyes. "You wish!"

"Andi!" Lorraine yelled as she walked out of her door with Roxie on her heels. "We need you!"

"Before I leave," Andi said. "I highly suggest you both go back to your condos and stay away from each other. You'll receive those restraining orders any minute now. The next time you're fighting in public like this, you're both going to jail. I won't be able to help either of you." She marched off quickly, wanting to get as far away from the bickering as possible. She met The Water Guppies in Lorraine's yard.

Lorraine looked even more like Mrs. Claus in her red velour jogging suit. "Someone broke into my home last night. It happened sometime after the séance, while I was at Roxie's. If we had come over earlier for my Richard Simmons' DVD, we might have run into the burglar. I'm too young to die!"

Roxie's sandals clicked on the concrete sidewalk. She would have looked like an ordinary grandmother in her white shorts and yellow T-shirt if it weren't for her mint-green, beehive hairdo. "They yanked the drawers out of her desk. There are file folders and papers all over the place. But once again, they left the flatscreen TV. Just saying, it's not your average burglar." She threw her hands up in the air as if unable to make any sense of the situation.

Andi was able to connect the dots. *If Brad broke in, he would have wanted to know if she had any evidence of his insider trading and who she shared the information with. He would also want to know if she had any access to any recordings made by the bug her cousin planted in his office.* "Do you have a computer?"

Lorraine shook her head. "Just a smartphone."

Andi glanced over her shoulder toward the girls. Emma was watching Nina retreat toward her condo. "Emma, can you come here?"

"Sure." The signs of anger faded as she grew closer. Once she reached the grandmas, she pushed a stray strand of blonde hair behind her ear and gazed over at them as innocent as could be. "What's up?"

"Someone broke into Lorraine's condo last night. I don't think Nina was the one you caught on your phone." She gestured toward the girl's sweater pocket. "Can I see that picture again?"

"Of course." Emma brought up the image on her phone and then handed it over.

"I'm sending it to my phone." Andi worked fast to complete the task and then showed the picture to Lorraine. "Does that tennis shoe look familiar?"

Lorraine stared at the picture. "I'm sorry. I can't even tell if the shoe belongs to a man or a woman."

Roxie snatched the phone. "Who wears white tennis shoes anymore? Don't they all have colorful lines or logos nowadays, so they can charge a mint for something that will fall apart in six months?"

"Maybe we can't see the logo on the shoe," Andi said. She reached for the phone and handed it back to Emma. "Which window did you take that picture from?"

Emma walked around the condo to show them. Nearby, they found Lorraine's bent window screen on the grass.

"I'm going to guess that this is where he, or she, got inside." *I'm still betting it was Brad.* Andi pulled her smartphone out of her jeans pocket and forwarded the picture of the tennis shoe to Lorraine's phone. "You should call the police and ask for the detective working Betsy's case."

"I have to go," Emma said. "I hope I've been some help."

"You have," Andi said. "Thanks."

Roxie waited for Emma to get out of hearing distance before lecturing Andi. "Lorraine *cannot* call that detective! He'll start to wonder what she has in common with Betsy besides strawberry margaritas at the pool."

Andi sighed. "I highly suggest you call the police *after* I leave, and the next time I see you, I don't want to know whether or not you actually followed my advice."

Roxie whispered to Lorraine, "She doesn't want to go to jail for withholding evidence."

"It's not *really* evidence," Lorraine said. "Besides, we already told her we're guilty of insider trading."

Roxie sighed. "But *you all* have hallucinations brought on by a combination of dementia and medical marijuana."

"We do?" Lorraine caught the wide-eyed look her friend sent her way. "Oh, yeah, we do. Andi, you can't believe anything The Water Guppies tell you."

Andi rubbed her temple. "I'll keep that in mind." She jerked her thumb over her shoulder. "I'm going to go back to my place to work on this case." She placed her hand on Lorraine's shoulder. "I'm going to do everything I can to find Betsy's murderer and put him behind bars."

"Thank you, dear." Lorraine patted Andi's hand. "Please be careful."

"You, too. Stay with Roxie." Andi rushed back to her condo. Once inside, she booted up her laptop and downloaded the security footage from Vera, their spy in the birdhouse. She studied the vehicles entering the complex the previous night. After eleven o'clock, the number dwindled to almost nothing. She slowly fast-forwarded the footage, growing more impatient by the second. *There has to be something here!*

She leaned her head on her hand and continued watching the footage. Movement in the dark, near the gate, caught her attention. She leaned closer and checked the time stamp—ten minutes to one. A man drove a dark car up to the gate and entered a code allowing him to come inside the complex. She created a computer screenshot and then used her phone to record the driver's actions. Besides wanting the evidence handy to share, she found it easier to zoom in on an object with her phone.

Pressing her fingers apart on the phone's screen, she enlarged the image of the bearded driver. "John? The bug guy?" She adjusted the picture again, but it still looked like him. "There's no good reason for him to be here in the middle of the night—unless there was something wrong with Poppy."

****

Andi couldn't get rid of the nagging feeling that something might have happened to Poppy. *Why else would her cousin visit her in the middle of the night?* When she finally decided to check for herself, she removed the baking class sign-up sheet from her desk drawer. She had already entered the number into her phone when she realized she couldn't tell Poppy how she knew her cousin had come onto the property in the middle of the night. The familiar voice answered on the third ring.

"Poppy, it's Andi. I hate to bother you." She stood and paced her dining room.

"No bother," Poppy replied through the phone. "I still have fifteen minutes before I have to leave for my class. What's up?" Her voice sounded carefree and friendly. Not sick at all.

"I just wanted to make sure you were all right." Andi stopped pacing. She stood next to her dining room table and spat out the closest version to the truth that she could risk telling. "Someone spotted your cousin driving onto the property in the middle of the night, and they were worried that something had happened to you."

A long pause followed.

"Hmm, I don't know what you're talking about," Poppy said, sounding confused. "My cousin wasn't here last night. Whoever thought they saw him was mistaken. John was in Tucson yesterday."

"Are you sure?"

"Positive. I spoke to my aunt last night, and she told me John was with her."

"I'm sorry to bother you with this misunderstanding, but I am glad you're okay." Andi stared at the picture of John on her laptop and wondered why Poppy was lying to her. "I'll let you know when we reschedule the baking lesson."

After the call, Andi dug through her junk drawer for

John's business card. The perforated edges caught her attention. *It looks like he made it with a printer.* It didn't take much effort to create your cards with a template and then print them on sheets of perforated cards available at the office supply store. The tricky part was separating them in a way that made them appear professionally made.

She returned to her laptop and searched for Arizona Bug Hunters, the name of John's pesticide company. A simple website popped up. She had thought for sure he would turn out to be a fake. Her gut told her to keep searching. *I could run over to his shop and snoop around after Luke gets off work. He'll want to come along. He could claim he wanted to negotiate a contract for the complex.*

Luke had a navigation system in his car, but she wanted to know the general location of where they were going. She typed the address from the website into her laptop and ran a search. To her surprise, the picture that hit her screen was a burger joint, not a pesticide company. *What?* She picked up her phone and called the number listed in the upper right corner.

"Zoda's Burgers and Shakes," said a high-pitched voice.

"What is your address?" Andi listened to the employee rattle off the same address listed on John's website and business card. "How long have you been located there?"

"How long have we been here?!" the employee yelled to someone in the restaurant. Her voice sounded muffled on Andi's end. A moment later, the employee answered, "Eleven years."

"Thank you very much." Andi hung up and called Meg. "Are you in the mood to do surveillance?"

Five minutes later, Andi backed out onto the road. Meg ran out of her condo and jumped inside.

"I'm glad my boss insisted I take at least a week off after the car accident." Meg buckled up and then checked her reflection in the mirror attached to the sun visor. You couldn't tell she had recently been admitted to the hospital. "Who are we spying on?"

"Poppy." Andi shifted into drive and pressed down on the gas.

"Poppy? What did she do?"

"I think she lied to me. I just found out her cousin is a fake, and I'm willing to bet she is, too." Andi filled her in as she drove out of the complex and down the street to a strip mall parking lot. "When I called, Poppy said she was going to school. It that's true, she'll have to pass by here."

"You don't think she's a student at the veterinary school?"

"I think it's all a lie." Andi kept her gaze glued to the oncoming traffic. "But I do think she will drive out of our complex because she told me she was going to school. I suspect she called her cousin after we hung up, and they might meet to come up with a plan to cover their tracks."

The next few minutes passed by at a snail's pace.

Andi rubbed the tension gathering at her forehead. "I guess I was wrong. Poppy must have decided to stay home after all."

"There she is!" Meg pointed to a small compact car with the attractive redhead behind the wheel. Keeping her head facing forward, she drove by the strip mall without glancing in their direction.

Andi turned the engine over and shifted into reverse. When she reached the exit, she turned right and eased onto the street. Only two cars separated them from Poppy at the intersection. The light turned from red to green, and they all moved forward.

Meg leaned to the side and peered out through the front window. "Should we get closer, so we don't lose her?"

"I don't want to risk getting caught." Andi kept a safe distance behind until they reached the university. She slowed, not wanting to get too close. Poppy turned into the parking lot and traveled to the far end. The other two cars between them continued driving down the busy street.

Andi turned into the lot and selected a parking spot near the front of the building. "From here we'll be able to see if she goes inside."

"You still think she's not a student?"

Andi shrugged. "I don't know. Since he's a fake, I figured she must be, too. It looks like I'm wrong."

After another minute of waiting, Poppy walked out of

the parking lot and into the closest building. The heavy-looking backpack she wore made a convincing argument that she was attending class.

Meg turned in her seat to face Andi. "Do you think her cousin might meet her here?"

"I doubt it." Andi lifted her phone from the console. "Maybe the picture in the security footage wasn't him, but I could swear it was."

"That's good enough for me." Meg turned toward the building. "Doesn't it seem odd that he would lie about owning a pesticide company?"

"More than odd when you consider everything going on in our complex." Andi kept her eye on the building as well, just in case Poppy left or her cousin showed up. "I don't believe in coincidences. I wonder if Brad hired him to spy at the complex."

Meg's eyes widened. "Pretending to be a bug guy is a great cover. He would have a legitimate reason to walk the property and spy on everyone. You should remember that if you ever need a disguise."

"True." Andi typed her password into the website her sister used to run background searches. She entered Brad's name since he was the one who got Lorraine's cousin fired at Lincoln and Martin Investments. When the results popped up on the screen, she handed her phone to Meg. "Would you enter this address into the navigator?"

"Sure. I gather you want to talk to this Brad guy." Meg started typing the address into the car's screen. "Are you going to ask him if he hired John?"

Andi shifted into reverse. "Less talk and more spy."

"Good idea. He would only lie anyway."

It took them over forty minutes to reach the Scottsdale neighborhood. On the way, they tried to distract themselves with small talk about Andi's plans for her wedding. Meg had just located a list of top-ten wedding venues on her phone when the voice on the navigator instructed them to turn right in two hundred feet.

The mud-brown, ranch-style home and its two car garage, built too close to its neighbors, wasn't the type of house Andi had expected. "You would think a man guilty of insider trading could afford a mansion."

Meg tapped her chin with her finger. "Maybe he's keeping a low profile."

The house wasn't a dump. On the contrary, most people would find it inviting. A short sidewalk from the driveway led to a black, decorative gate mounted to two short pillars with pots filled with colorful pansies on top. The house just wasn't one of the multi-million dollar homes Scottsdale was known for. That didn't make it cheap.

Andi parked on the curb, three houses away from Brad's.

"Now what?" Meg asked.

She turned and spotted a dark sports car turning onto the street at the corner. "Duck!"

Meg unbuckled her seatbelt and slid to the floor. Even with her petite frame, it was a tight squeeze. "Are they gone yet?"

Andi listened. "I didn't hear anyone drive by." They remained silent for a minute, and then Andi heard the distinct sound of a garage door lifting. She snuck a peek out the side window and spotted the sports car pulling into the driveway. Unfortunately, she couldn't get a good look at the driver. "It's him. At least I think it is since he's entering Brad's garage."

"How long do we have to stay down here?" Meg sat on her knees on the floorboard. At least she wore comfortable-looking slacks and a loose-fitting blouse.

"Until he goes inside." She peered out the window again and spotted a man leaving the garage and walking toward the sidewalk in front of the house. "Down!"

"I am down," Meg griped.

"Sorry." Andi listened again as she tried to make herself smaller in her seat. The sound of footsteps sounded louder. "He's walking down the sidewalk on his side of the street."

"They have a community mailbox center up ahead," Meg whispered. "As long as he sticks to that sidewalk, we should be okay. I would hate for him to glance down into the car and spot us."

"That would be embarrassing," Andi said, keeping her

voice low. "We could always yell surprise! It's your half-birthday!"

Meg chuckled. Once the footsteps sounded closer to the mail center and further away from the car, she snuck a peek. "He's wearing white tennis shoes—like the ones in the picture you showed me."

Andi heard the sound of someone opening a mailbox and decided it was time to take a look. She had to see if his shoes matched the one in Emma's picture. She lifted her head and noticed a man with a beard pulling envelopes out of the box.

Recognition hit Andi like a two-by-four to the face. Her jaw dropped, and she ducked back down. "Brad is John or John is Brad!"

"What?!" Meg lifted her head and then dropped back down onto the floorboard. "I never saw Poppy's cousin. Are you sure it's him?"

"Positive!" Andi kept to a whisper as she explained. "On Lincoln's website, Brad is clean-cut, but the man standing at the mailbox has a beard like John." She felt her eyes widen. "It is John! I didn't realize it before because I never studied his face—other than noticing he was cute. Brad let his hair grow out several inches since the picture for the company website was taken. The beard also covered most of his facial features."

"If he's an investor, how did he get the pesticide equipment? Including the van?"

"He could have borrowed or even stolen it." Andi tried to stretch her aching leg, which was almost impossible scrunched down in the seat.

"Can you search for stolen vans from pesticide companies?"

"My sister could make some calls to the police station, but I don't want to involve her in all of this until she comes back from her vacation."

"When is that?" Meg asked while shifting her weight to one side.

"The end of next week."

"And you want this all wrapped up by then."

Andi nodded. "It would be easier to tell her I worked a

free case for Roxie if I have the bonus check in my hand from Gladys's daughter for proving her mother's innocence." She heard the sound of footsteps again and lifted her finger to her lips to signal Meg to be silent.

Once the garage door closed, they both checked to make sure the coast was clear.

Meg returned to her seat. "I understand he killed Lorraine's cousin because he had bugged Brad's office and knew the truth about his crimes. What I don't understand is why he killed Betsy, assuming he's the one who did it. There is still the chance Gladys did."

Andi sighed. "We have a lot more questions than answers, and the biggest question is, how do we put this guy away without implicating The Water Guppies?"

"I have no clue."

She turned the key in the ignition and then drove down the street. "I think we need to have another talk with Poppy. I'm not sure she knows the truth about her cousin. I might have misjudged her."

"What are you going to tell her?"

"I don't know yet."

****

An hour later, Andi and Meg filled Lorraine in on John being Brad or Brad being John. They had come up with a plan on the drive back, but they needed The Water Guppy's help to pull it off. The three of them walked silently to Poppy's condo. Lorraine kept wiping the nervous sweat off her palms onto her slacks.

Andi crossed her fingers for good luck and then knocked on Poppy's door.

The veterinarian student opened on the third knock and poked her head outside. "Andi?" Her gaze traveled to the others and then she stepped out onto the stoop. "Did I do something wrong?"

"Of course not," Andi said. "Why would you ask that?"

"It looks like you brought the HOA board with you."

Lorraine laughed. "You wouldn't catch me dead on that board."

Andi lifted her brows to remind The Guppy that they were on the HOA board and might take offense.

Lorraine pressed her lips together and looked contrite.

"We were walking laps around the complex," Meg said.

"Exercise," Lorraine explained. "And while we were walking, we spotted a few anthills."

"And I remembered I lost your cousin's card," Andi said. "I need to schedule him to come back out to spray. We have a bigger ant problem than I knew."

"Oh," Poppy's expression softened. "I'm out of cards, but I'll ask him to call you."

"Okay..." Andi turned to Lorraine, who was supposed to speak next.

"Your cousin is quite handsome," the Water Guppy said.

Poppy smiled. "He takes after our grandfather."

"By any chance, was your cousin an investment banker at Lincoln and Martin?" Lorraine asked. "I had a relative who worked there, and I swear I saw your cousin during one of my visits. He had his own office and everything! He must have been important!"

Poppy hesitated. "I don't know if he wants it to be common knowledge, but he did work there." She pressed her lips together. "The stress got to be too much for him. Finally, a friend suggested he open his own business and offered to mentor him. John likes that he can set his own hours, and he's proud of the fact that he only uses all-natural ingredients to repel insects."

"That is truly something to be proud of," Meg said with a smile. "How long has he owned his company?"

"About six months now."

"When did he leave Lincoln and Martin?" Andi asked.

"Five months ago." Poppy creased her brow. "Why all the questions?"

"We're nosy old ladies," Lorraine said with a chuckle.

"We've taken enough of your time." Andi backed off the porch, hoping to keep Poppy from getting too suspicious. "Before I forget, we also stopped by to tell you that we rescheduled the baking lesson for tomorrow night at seven. I hope you can make it."

"I wouldn't miss it." Poppy still looked confused when she shut her door.

Andi's mind raced with thoughts on the silent walk back to Lorraine's condo. They gathered on her stoop.

"What do you think?" Meg asked.

Andi crossed her arms over her chest. "I think Lorraine's cousin couldn't have been fired for stealing money out of Brad's desk if Brad had quit and didn't have a desk."

"That's a very good point." Lorraine glanced back at Poppy's condo. "So is she lying or being lied to?"

"I have no clue," Andi said. "I'm going to have to check into her background as well."

Lorraine placed her hand on Andi's arm. "You need to put that Brad guy behind bars for killing my cousin, even if it means giving the police the evidence they need to throw me in jail, too."

Andi's gut twisted. "I hope it doesn't come to that.

NINE

A half-hour after leaving Lorraine, Andi opened a bottle of Moscato. She hoped a few hours of relaxation might help her come up with a plan—an amazing plan. One that would keep The Water Guppies out of prison. She wanted that for herself, as well. If Detective Franks discovered she had kept evidence from him, he would throw the book at her.

"Half or full glass?"

"Need you ask?" Meg called out from the living room. She sounded as tired as Andi felt.

Andi carried two generous servings of the sweet wine into the living room and handed one to Meg, who sat at one end of the sofa.

"I hope this helps us come up with a plan," Meg said.

"If not, it will at least help us relax." With exhaustion setting in, Andi placed her glass on the table and then claimed the other end of the sofa. "The pizza will be here in forty minutes."

"I hope it arrives early." Meg kicked off her shoes and curled her legs up under her body without spilling a single drop of wine. "I could eat a large pepperoni all by myself."

"You usually can." Andi smiled as she leaned against a throw pillow. "I ordered two just in case Luke's mother cancels her dinner plans with him. She does that when she's not feeling well."

"Is that often?" Concern flickered through Meg's expression.

"Not so much," Andi said. "But I'm a planner, which brings me back to tonight's homework." She reached for her wine glass on the coffee table. "I know that Brad guy is the murderer. I just don't know how to prove it."

Meg took a sip of her Moscato. "What would that TV detective do? Get Brad to confess?"

Andi swirled the wine in her glass while she considered her favorite television mystery series. "He makes it look easy, and it's not. We would have to set a trap, and hope Brad is dumb enough to fall into it."

"That's all?" Meg rolled her eyes. "That should be a cinch," she said, with a heavy dose of sarcasm.

"I wish it were like a television show. They don't use real bullets." Andi examined the contents of her glass. "Maybe more wine will help me think out of the box. We need a plan he won't see through." They finished their wine, and Andi topped them off again. She placed the empty bottle down on the coffee table and said, "We know he's afraid someone will report him to the police."

"He could be afraid Lorraine's cousin recorded the information he got off the bug in Brad's office. A tape of Brad talking to the person who gave him the insider information would be hard to fight in court," Meg said. "He could also be afraid one of The Water Guppies will name him if she's arrested for insider trading."

Andi pictured those scenarios. "All of the above. He might also be afraid Lorraine has a copy of a tape." She took a sip of her wine and played with a thought. "I think I have a plan. It's not original, but I think it will work. Lorraine could tell Brad she had access to a recording her cousin made when he bugged his office and that she made several copies. If anything happens to her, or her friends, a copy will be sent to the police, the Federal Trade Commission, and the local news stations."

"Intriguing..." Meg ran her finger around the rim of her glass. "What if he demands proof?"

"Lorraine can claim he isn't in a position to demand anything."

Meg grinned. "She could tell him his time would be better spent moving out of the state."

"That could work." Worry nagged at Andi's gut. "But if it doesn't, he might try to kill Lorraine."

"He already tried to kill her—twice!"

"True." Andi rubbed the tension gathering at the back of her neck. "But I hate giving him another reason to try."

"It's her life," Meg said. "If it were me, I would want to try to take him down."

"You're right." Andi placed her glass back down on the table and stood. "We should run this idea by Lorraine."

"If she agrees to it, I know a messenger company that can take a letter over to his house in the morning."

"The sooner, the better." Andi grabbed her phone off the dining room table. "Who knows what that man is planning to do next."

****

The next morning, Andi and Meg stood in the entrance to Roxie's home, carrying her leather computer bag at her side. Andi had never entered Roxie's condo before. Not that she knew what waited for her inside. The way the zany woman dressed led her to predict her home would reflect a combined mix of the tastes of Elton John and Dolly Parton—different and interesting.

What Andi feared was the unexpected. You never knew what a woman who shoved recently lit cigarettes down into her bra would shove into her cupboards, fridge, or shower. There could be new strains of bacteria or mold growing in there, along with the heavy stench of cigarettes hanging in the air.

Andi and Meg followed Roxie into the dining room, where they found a formal Queen Anne dining room set. The cabinet displayed china with gold trim. Andi's jaw dropped open. This was the type of dining room set her conservative mother always wanted but never dared to own because she had raised three daughters who acted more like rough and tumbling football players—thanks to their father. After seeing this set, she would ask her sisters to chip in so they could buy it for their mother.

They slowly stepped into the living room, which looked more like Roxie. Andi rounded the four-tiered chandelier hanging in the center of the small space. She almost ran into a floor-to-ceiling picture of Elvis wearing his white and gold jumpsuit. *That explains her love of jumpsuits.* She backed up and joined Meg on the blue velour sofa. Roxie stood next to a flat-screen television mounted to the wall.

After taking a deep breath, Andi spelled out to Roxie and Lorraine the details of their plan. Martha and Irene were out shopping, which was probably a good idea. The fewer involved, the better.

Lorraine rocked nervously back and forth in an oak rocking chair with a dusty rose-colored velour cushion. "I think it's a good idea to tell Brad there's a tape proving he's guilty of insider trading, I just don't believe he will leave me alone if I threaten to have the tape released in the event anything happens to me." Lorraine cringed and rubbed her shoulders. "Guys like him kidnap and torture little old ladies like me to get what they want."

"Over my dead body!" Roxie removed her pearl-handled pistol from her bra. "Minnie Pearl will blast his—"

"Nobody is blasting anybody!" Andi leaned back against the sofa and held her breath, while Roxie pretended to shoot the television. "Please put that away!"

She shrugged and tugged at the top of her zebra-print jumpsuit.

"*Not* in your bra!" In an obvious attempt to avoid a misfiring, Meg scooted onto the arm of the sofa and then fell to the carpet below.

Andi jumped up and helped Meg to her feet. "Roxie, we are leaving if you don't put that gun in a purse or your bedroom!"

Roxie rolled her eyes. "You call yourself a detective? You're afraid of your own shadow."

Lorraine rubbed her face. "Roxie, they're afraid you'll accidentally kill someone. Now, do as they say."

"I have the safety on." When faced with a room of determined women, Roxie gave in with a huff of breath to

show her displeasure. "Okay, I'll put it in a purse—later."
She placed it on the glass coffee table. "Happy?"

"Yes, I am. Thank you." Andi said. The others breathed
easier as she continued. "We should start with a letter to
Brad. After that, we can come up with step two."

"I already have step two." Roxie pulled the listening
device out of her bra. "I say we find a place to hide outside
his house when he receives the message. If Poppy's in on
it, he'll call her right away."

"That's not a bad idea." Andi unzipped her bag,
removed her laptop, and then booted it up on the glass
coffee table. "We need a perfect letter." She opened a
document page and began typing. "To Brad."

"You're using business format in a threat letter?"
Lorraine stopped rocking in the chair.

Andi stopped typing. "It's not a friendly letter."

"Good point." The Guppy returned to rapidly rocking
back and forth.

Andi returned to typing. "My cousin caught every word
you said."

Meg added with dramatic flair, "Make one wrong move,
and your picture will be on the five o'clock news."

Andi glanced over at her with a grin.

"Type that," Meg said, motioning for her to get back to
work.

"Oh," Lorraine said. "Tell him you have a dozen copies
of what he said ready to be delivered to people who will
make him wish he were *dead*."

"I'll change *dead* to living in South America," Andi said.
"I don't want his mind thinking about death."

"Good idea," Meg whispered.

"Yeah," Lorraine said. "We all know who he would want
to kill." She removed her phone from her designer purse.
"I'll call the messenger service. Meg, what's the number?"

"I have a better idea," Roxie said. She removed her
phone from her bra, tapped in a number, and then held the
phone to her ear.

Andi cringed. *Note to self. Never use that woman's
phone.*

"Buddy." Roxie's voice softened when she spoke to her

son. "You're too busy to help your mother?" Pause. "That can wait. I need you to run an errand for me. And pack a revolver just in case."

Meg's eyes widened. "A revolver?"

"He needs protection," Roxie told them. "We don't want Brad killing the messenger. He's my son." She snapped her phone shut and shoved it back into her bra. "We should make Brad sign for the delivery, and then bag the paper and pen in case we need DNA or fingerprints."

"I like the way you think." Lorraine gave her an energetic high-five. For a moment, the worry had left Lorraine's Mrs. Claus-looking face, but it returned quickly.

"It can't hurt." Andi typed a delivery slip, using the name of a real messenger service, and then saved both documents to a thumb drive. She then passed it along to Roxie, who left the room and later returned with printed pages. Andi sealed the letter in an envelope she'd brought with her and handed both to Roxie.

A loud rap at the door announced Buddy's arrival. Andi remembered him as a hundred-pound amateur botanist. When he stepped inside, she did a double-take. He'd grown a handle-bar mustache and his straight, dark hair now reached his shoulders.

"Ladies." He lifted the tan, felt cowboy hat off his head in greeting.

Andi waved as her gaze took in his leather jacket, jeans, and cowboy boots.

Roxie told him what they wanted to accomplish while she led him outside with a hand on his shoulder. Next, she handed him the envelope, delivery slip, and a pen. "If he asks you any questions, tell him you know nothing. You're only there to deliver the letter."

Andi followed them outside. "Make sure he signs the slip. He needs to think you work for a legitimate delivery service."

Buddy straddled his motorcycle, slipped the paperwork and pen into his inside jacket pocket, and then zipped it shut. The four women stood on the grass near the bike.

"Text me when you get home," Roxie said. "And make sure no one follows you. Take the scenic route."

"Not a problem." He gunned the engine and smoke bellowed out the exhaust pipe when he took off.

Lorraine stepped out of the condo and removed a set of car keys from her handbag. "My SUV won't stick out like a sore thumb in a residential neighborhood." She walked swiftly to the next-door neighbor's car and peeled a magnetic real estate sign from the driver's side door. "I called and asked if I could borrow this after Roxie said she wanted to spy on Brad."

"That's a great cover!" Andi said. Their plan was falling into place. "I'm going to order all kinds of commercial signs for our detective agency."

"I noticed when we left his house last time that it backs up to a grassy retention area," Meg said. "We should park there. The neighbors will think we are visiting with someone who is thinking of selling their house, but they won't know who. If we park in front of someone's house, a nosey neighbor might call them."

"We don't want that happening," Andi said. "Meg, you direct Lorraine while she drives." For the first time since they had come up with their plan, Andi felt like it might succeed.

****

Forty minutes later, they parked in front of a grassy area with a basin in the middle. It looked like a small meteor had hit the corner of the block, and then the residents chose to plant grass on top. The rest of the neighborhood had been built at a slight incline, so rainwater traveled down the street to the retention park. The basin would fill with water, preventing flooding to the surrounding houses. New housing developments in flood zones required proactive measurements.

Brad's house was the second one backing up to the retention park. Andi scanned the area before unlocking the back door of the SUV.

"Lorraine, stay here and play lookout." Andi didn't want The Water Guppy getting caught by this guy. There was no telling what he might do.

Lorraine looked back at her through the rearview mirror with wide eyes. "Lookout for what?"

"Police, nosey neighbors, Brad walking the neighborhood," Andi said, remaining in her seat with one hand on the door handle.

The color drained from The Water Guppy's face.

"I'll stay with her," Meg said.

"Good idea." Andi mouthed, *Thank you*. In a louder voice, she said, "Let's put our phones on vibrate."

"Done." Roxie pushed open her door. "Let's get this show on the road." With her small stature, she had to slide out of the SUV and then land on her stilettos. When she regained her balance, she wiggled and tugged at her clothes to get everything inside of her jumpsuit back where it belonged. Roxie's green outfit with silver starbursts was probably her idea of camouflage.

Andi followed her over the grassy park and then between Brad's backyard wall and his neighbor's. The roar of a motorcycle invaded the neighborhood and grew louder as it came closer. She felt the phone vibrate on her hip and read Meg's text. "Buddy just drove by," Andi whispered to Roxie.

She answered with her *no-duh* expression.

Quietly, they continued walking between the houses until they neared Brad's kitchen. They suddenly heard children squealing inside the neighbor's house.

"Let's stop here," Andi whispered.

They both eased down onto the grass and leaned against the brick wall. Roxie landed with a gentle thud.

She watched the wacky woman reach inside of her jumpsuit top to remove the listening device. This time, Andi was prepared. She removed latex gloves from her pocket and tugged them on her hands. Next, she removed a package containing a disinfecting wipe and ripped it open.

Roxie frowned. "Really?"

Andi pressed her lips together and nodded. After disinfecting the earbud, she inserted it into her ear. She had to focus on blocking out the neighbor's kids playing or the noise would prove to be too much of a distraction.

The listening device made Buddy's distinctive footsteps

on the driveway sound close. He knocked and a few seconds later, someone opened the door.

Brad didn't sound surprised when he learned he had a certified letter. He signed for it, and Roxie's son left without incident. Then Brad ripped open the envelope and everything changed.

"Who does she think she is?!" Brad threw something that shattered on impact.

Roxie ducked as if the object had been thrown at her and then sent Andi a look that said they had better not get caught.

"Answer the phone!" Brad ranted a string of obscenities.

Andi thought she heard a woman's voice, but it was too faint to tell for sure.

"Put Operation Eraser into effect," Brad ordered. "And call me when you get this."

When Andi heard the distinct sound of car keys, she yanked the listening device out of her ear and handed it to Roxie. "Keep it in your pocket like a normal person," she whispered.

"It *is* my pocket." She shoved it back down her bra as they rushed to the end of the backyard walls and into the retention park.

Andi's legs felt sore from sitting on the hard, cold ground. She glanced back to check on Roxie and found her wobbly on her heels. Concerned, Andi wrapped her arm around the older woman's back and helped her rush across the grass.

Meg spotted them and ushered Lorraine back to her car with a hand to her back.

When Brad's car sped around the corner, Andi and Roxie both dropped to the grass inside the basin of the retention area, while Lorraine and Meg hid behind the passenger side of the SUV. The way he kept speeding out of the neighborhood gave Andi the impression he hadn't seen them.

All four women rushed to get back to the vehicle. Andi helped Roxie up the side of the basin and didn't let go of her arm until they reached the sidewalk beside the SUV.

"Where to?" Lorraine pulled the seatbelt across her body and snapped the lock into place.

"Follow him," Andi said. "But not too close."

"Take her advice," Roxie said. "That man is possessed. He'll annihilate us all if he sees us."

"Oh, great!" Lorraine's sarcasm hung in the air as she leaned forward over the wheel and shifted into drive. To her credit, she did remain three car lengths behind him, but she did ride the bumper of a black sedan in front of them. The driver eventually moved over to the middle lane. Lorraine then rode the bumper of a flower delivery van in front of her. Andi worried the driver would move over, and Brad would spot them.

"You can pull back now," Andi said.

"Pull back?" Lorraine glanced toward the back seat. "I'm not driving a horse."

Roxie sighed. "She means to slow down."

"Why didn't she say so?" Lorraine slowed to a snail's pace.

Meg, sitting in the passenger seat, shifted to see Andi in the back. "We're going to lose him!"

Brad turned on a familiar road.

"No, we're not," Andi said. "He's headed to our complex."

"What!?" Lorraine swerved the car on the road. "He's going there to kill me!"

This is all my fault. It doesn't matter that Lorraine wanted me to do anything I could to put this guy behind bars. I should have known something would go wrong. Once they reached a residential neighborhood near their complex, Andi pointed to a corner house. "Pull over!"

"Why?" Roxie furrowed her brow. "We're going to lose him!"

"Pull over! We know where he's going."

Lorraine turned the corner and parked along the curb. Once she'd stopped, she turned around to face Andi and Roxie. "Now what?"

Andi could see the fear on her face. She yanked on the side door. "I'm getting out, and the rest of you are going to the mall until I call to tell you the coast is clear."

"You're not leaving without me!" Meg jumped out the front passenger side door.

"I'm coming, too." Roxie climbed out after her. "You need me. I'm meaner than both of you." She slid to the ground, then wiggled and tugged at her clothes until they were back in place again.

"I'll be waiting at the mall's food court," Lorraine said. "I'm going to eat my way from one end to the other while I wait for your call."

Roxie shoved her door shut, and Lorraine sped away.

Andi sighed as she watched her go. *I have to make this right for everyone.* "Let's go. The front gate isn't far."

"I have a better idea." Roxie placed a quick call. "Hey, big guy." Her voice took on a flirtatious tone. "We need your cart again." Pause. "Yes, we're on another case." Pause. "We'll be outside the front gate."

An uneasy mood settled over the group as they walked toward the complex. A few minutes later, a cart driven by Roxie's unrequited love interest, came speeding toward them. The Cowboy drove faster than Andi would have thought possible in the electrically-charged vehicle.

The Cowboy, who used to own a ranch, sported a tan to go along with the age spots. He spent a lot of time at the pool, drinking low-calorie beer while listening to country-western music.

When he reached them, he made a quick U-turn. "Hop on, ladies."

Roxie pushed Meg out of the way and climbed onto the front seat. "We're in a hurry!" she told him. "We have another bad guy to catch!"

Andi leaned forward on the bench seat. "We need to know where this guy has gone *without* him seeing us."

"He's probably at Lorraine's place or his cousin Poppy's," Meg said. "She lives in the old Stewart condo."

"Got it." He sped toward the front gate, then pushed in his code on the keypad. It took an eternity for the metal gate to slowly swing open. When it did, The Cowboy eased inside.

Everyone looked both ways to make sure the coast was clear. "Go!" they all whisper-yelled in chorus.

He raced straight toward the clubhouse. Instead of parking, he drove onto the sidewalk that led to the pool and then cut through the center of the complex toward the fountain on the other side. The three women scanned the area for Brad's car.

When The Cowboy neared the back of Lorraine's condo, Andi patted his shoulder. "Stop here. I'll be right back."

She hopped off with Meg following behind. They ran between Lorraine and Emma's condos, glancing inside as they moved from one window to the other. Once they reached the front, they both scanned the road for Brad's car and then ran back to the golf cart.

"He's not there!" Meg hopped back on, forcing the cart to rock back and forth.

"Let's check Poppy's place," Andi said.

The Cowboy sped off again. When they reached the fountain, he slowed. Meg and Andi crept off near the bushes to hide. This time, they spotted Brad's car in front of his cousin's condo.

"Now what?" Meg asked.

"Follow me." Andi crept back to the cart. "Roxie, I need the listening device." She blew out a long, slow breath as she watched the woman pull it out of her bra. "And I'm keeping it this time," Andi added.

Roxie shrugged and turned to The Cowboy with admiring eyes. "Where should *we* hide?"

He turned to Andi for guidance.

"Park behind the bushes, and if he leaves, follow him without letting him see you." Andi made sure there weren't any neighbors around before she crossed the road with Meg at her side. They ran between Poppy's condo and her neighbor's. "The rear window," Andi directed Meg.

They dropped to the cold grass and sat cross-legged, leaning against the wall. Andi wiped off the device and handed one end to Meg. They inserted the buds into their ears and then listened closely. Silence greeted them. After another minute, Andi grew impatient.

"I don't think Poppy is there," Meg whispered.

"One way to find out. I'll try her phone." Andi removed

her cell phone from her pocket and placed the call.

Meg shook her head. "I don't hear any ringing sounds inside the condo."

Andi then placed her phone on vibrate in case Poppy returned her call at the worst possible moment. She'd seen that happen too many times on detective shows. "Let's check all the windows."

They walked around the condo and peered in wherever they could. Poppy had little in the way of furnishings—about as much as Mack. Only she decorated with more colors than brown. Andi did notice that all of the lights were off, and nothing moved. If Brad was inside, he was hiding, and that didn't make sense.

Meg shrugged. "Maybe Poppy took him somewhere."

"Maybe." The garage didn't have any windows, so they couldn't be sure if Poppy's car was parked inside. "Let's go!"

They scanned the neighborhood before crossing the road again, careful to make sure Brad wasn't around.

Andi shook her head when they neared the cart. "He's not there."

"He'll be back," The Cowboy said. "His car is here."

"I hope he doesn't wait too long." Meg climbed back into her seat. "I'm getting hungry."

"You're always hungry," Roxie complained.

"I eat when I'm stressed." Meg narrowed her eyes and glared in a *leave me alone* expression, and then added, "Maybe Lorraine can bring us chili fries from the food court."

Andi leaned against the golf cart's back seat and shook her head. "We are trying to keep her out of harm's way."

"Can we order take out at a stake out?" Meg chuckled. "That rhymes."

"My son can bring us something," Roxie said. "How about a pizza?" She gazed up at The Cowboy with a big smile and said, "I bet you're a pepperoni man."

Andi rolled her eyes. "You all wait here and figure out your order. I'm going to search the complex." She walked briskly from the cart and toward the pool. When she reached the fence, she turned right, making sure to keep her eyes open for Brad.

A shuffling noise behind her made her jump. She found Meg running from tree to tree until she caught up.

"What are you doing here?" Andi leaned against the trunk of a pine, waiting for an answer. "I thought you were hungry."

"The pizza won't be here for thirty minutes." Meg motioned for her to continue. "Let's find this guy."

Suddenly, an adorable beagle darted around a bush with a red, nylon leash dragging behind him.

"Snoops, come back here!" Alicia Kozak, another one of their new neighbors, stepped out from behind a tree. When she spotted Andi and Meg, she rushed forward and scooped the dog up into her arms. Her long-sleeved white shirt and gray pencil skirt gave the impression that she may have come home from work to walk her dog. "I hope he didn't cause any trouble. You can see I had him on a leash. He got away."

"No worries." Andi smiled and patted the dog's head. She suspected the comment about the leash was her way of letting the president of the homeowners' association know she was following the rules. Andi wished the neighbors would stop talking to her like she walked around the property with a clipboard, marking down who was naughty and nice.

"What a cutie," Andi directed her comment to the dog, who was trying to wiggle his way out of his owner's arms.

When Alicia moved in, Andi had welcomed her to the neighborhood. The thirty-something brunette with wavy hair seemed nice enough, but she always changed the conversation when Andi brought up her past. No one in the community knew where Alicia had come from or why she had moved to Euphoria Lane.

Meg patted his back, and he licked her face. She pulled back, laughing. "How long have you had him?"

"Awhile. I better go." She lowered him to the grass and directed him away with the leash.

Andi didn't expect the introvert to be of any help with their current situation, but she needed to ask. "By any chance, have you seen a man with a beard walking around the complex?"

Alicia turned back toward them, and apprehension flickered across her face. She hesitated and then finally nodded. "He was near the dumpster in the corner." She pointed toward the section of the complex where Andi lived.

"Thanks," Meg said. She jerked her head toward the direction they needed to go. "Let's go!"

"Thanks a lot." Andi wasted no time in following her friend, wondering why Alicia didn't want to tell her about Brad.

They raced between several buildings until they reached the side of the road. Andi could see her condo from where they stood. All of a sudden, Brad came running out of her front door with Mack chasing after him.

Andi felt her eyes widen in surprise. *What were they doing in my condo?!*

"Stop! Federal Investigator!" Mack yelled at Brad.

"Federal what?" Andi turned to Meg. "Mack's a fed?"

Meg's jaw dropped, and her mouth formed a big oval shape, but no words escaped.

Brad ran toward the homes across the road from where Andi and Meg stood. Mack chased after him. He ran faster than Andi would have imagined he could and would probably catch up, but she wasn't about to stand around and watch the show. She had to make sure Brad didn't escape. She ran toward him, hoping to cut him off.

Andi was ten feet away when Mack passed her and jumped on top of Brad's back.

A shot rang out, and both men tumbled to the asphalt road.

What the... Andi ran behind the closest tree for cover. Meg caught up with her as another shot rang out.

The tree wasn't wide enough to protect them. Andi pointed toward their neighbor's red SUV parked in a driveway, and they both ran for their lives. They practically dived behind the vehicle and then dropped to their knees.

Meg held onto the bumper and breathed heavily. "Who's shooting?"

"Roxie?" Andi shook the thought away. "I don't know.

Maybe her son, Buddy." Not knowing for sure ate at her. "It could be anybody."

"Maybe it's the police," Meg said. "But I thought they had to announce who they are."

"Mack already did—sort of." Andi wished she could take back her words the second they escaped her mouth.

Meg looked stricken. "I can't believe Mack lied to us. To me..."

Andi had no words to comfort her. The man had committed one of the worst sins as far as Meg was concerned.

The gunshots stopped, but Andi wasn't about to risk leaving the safety of their hiding place. She listened and waited until a man stepped around the vehicle. Panic caught in her throat.

"It's all clear," Mack said. His expression held the confidence his position demanded, but his eyes shifted to show the guilt he felt over deceiving them. "You can come out now."

"Where's Brad?" Andi feared she already knew the answer.

He shook his head. "Dead."

"The shooter?" Meg asked.

"Gone."

"So it wasn't the police?" Andi pushed against the bumper to stand.

"No. I'm afraid not."

Andi offered her hand, but Meg remained on the concrete pulling her knees closer to her chest.

Mack lowered himself to her level. "Are you okay?"

"No!" Meg shook her head. The betrayal she felt showed in her expression. "Someone shot real bullets, and you lied to me. You're not a retired dentist. You're a fed."

"Not exactly," he said.

"Not exactly what?" Meg demanded.

"I am retired...but not from dentistry. I'm working for the agency temporarily—like an independent contractor."

Meg narrowed her eyes. "Contractor?"

"I can't explain until this assignment is over." He wiped the sweat beading at his brow despite the cool weather. "I was asked to come out of retirement for a few months."

She rolled her eyes. "I bet you're not even from Chicago."

"That part is true, but I didn't move here recently. I retired here six months ago."

"You haven't been living in Euphoria that long," Meg said. You could almost see her thoughts churning.

"The feds rented a condo for him," Andi guessed.

He glanced up at her. "I own a house about five miles away."

Everything fell into place. The feds needed to plant Mack in Euphoria Condominiums to spy on people who live here—The Water Guppies.

Andi was about to grab Meg and pull her away when she remembered Brad had come running from her condo. "What were you doing inside my condo?"

"I spotted this guy breaking in, and I caught him messing with your stove."

"My stove?!" The thought of her home blowing up made her pulse race and her eyes widen in panic.

"It's okay," he said. "I turned it off before I chased him out."

"Why would he try to kill me?"

Meg glanced up at her. "He had to know you were investigating Betsy's death and Lorraine's attempted murder." She started to stand, and when Mack swiftly rose and reached his hand out to help, she slapped it away. "I don't need help from liars."

He backed away, and the sound of sirens in the distance grew louder. At that moment, The Cowboy and Roxie pulled up behind the SUV. They both climbed off the cart and stared at the body.

"Looks like he won't be bothering anyone ever again." Roxie whistled. "Good job, Andi. I didn't know you had it in you."

"I didn't shoot him!" Andi threw her arms up in the air. "I don't even own a gun."

"Your sister has one," Roxie said.

"True, but I don't use it. I wouldn't."

"Who killed him?" The Cowboy asked.

"We don't know," Meg said. "Ask the fed." She gestured towards Mack.

"Fed?" Roxie raked her eyes over Mack. "Maybe in a past life."

"He came out of retirement," Andi said.

The Cowboy guffawed. "They don't do that."

Andi made direct eye contact with Roxie and said, "They do if they were once federal investigators and were asked to work a special case that needed someone old enough to retire."

"They would send old men to spy on..." Roxie backed up to the cart. "I have somewhere I need to go."

Food court, Andi mouthed to Roxie. *Get Lorraine out of here.*

****

Two hours after the police interviewed her, Andi taped another *Baking Class Cancelled* sign on the clubhouse door. She dropped the tape dispenser back into her canvas bag, spun on her heel, and found Mack standing in her way.

She frowned and stiffened her stance. "What do you want?"

"You have every right to be upset with me," he said matter-of-factly.

He was there to investigate The Water Guppies. Of course she had every right to be upset. "Tell me something I don't already know."

"Brad doesn't have a cousin named Poppy. He doesn't have *any* female cousins." He waited for her take in this new piece of information and respond.

"Do you think she shot him?"

"I do." He glanced back over his shoulder before speaking as if making sure no one was around to overhear their conversation. "I have to believe you know what is going on here."

"I—"

"Just listen for a minute. Brad's job didn't give him access to the kind of information needed to commit these

134

crimes. He had help."

She wanted to tell him that Lorraine's cousin had overheard Brad talking to someone else, and that was how he knew Brad was involved in insider trading, but she didn't want to say anything that would provide information that could be used against Lorraine. He moved into the condo because he knew the grandma was involved. He most likely had evidence against her, but Andi didn't know what it was, and she wasn't going to add anything.

"Was Poppy in a position to help Brad commit his crime?"

He nodded.

"And you're telling me this because..."

"You need to warn your friends."

"She probably killed Brad, which means she's tying up loose ends, so The Water Guppies' lives are in danger." She looked to him for verification. He only blinked, and goosebumps traveled over her arms. "I'm going to find a safe place for them to hide," she said. "I don't want you to think they left to evade law enforcement."

"I understand. As long as you keep your cell phone on so I can reach you, I'll know you're not trying to help them leave the country."

She could do that. "Thank you for the warning. I know you might be going out on a limb for us."

"It's the right thing to do." He turned and walked away with a wide stride.

Andi removed her cell phone from her pocket and called Roxie. She answered on the first ring.

"I hope this is good news for a change." Roxie's voice sounded like a child's whine.

"We need to get The Water Guppies out of town!" Andi walked quickly across the road. "They need an overnight bag and enough clothes to last a few days."

"Why?"

"I'll tell you when I pick you all up at your place in fifteen minutes."

"Fifteen minutes?!"

"Fourteen now. Be ready." Andi passed the tree with the birdhouse and made a note to call Luke and have him check the security footage to see if Poppy was on the property when Brad was shot.

"I'm hiding them in Ida's condo," Roxie said. "Ida is away on the cruise, and I have her keys."

"I'll be there in thirteen minutes." Andi hung up and called Meg. "Can Chad stay at a friend's house for a few days?"

"Sure, why?"

"We need to get The Water Guppies away from here." Andi quickened her pace over the sidewalk to her condo. "Poppy isn't Brad's cousin. The police think she killed him. That means she's tying up loose ends, and she knows all about The Water Guppies." Andi unlocked her door and rushed to her master bedroom.

"There's six of us. We'll need my SUV. I'll pick you up in twenty minutes."

"Twelve." Andi hung up, opened her closet door, and grabbed her Go Bag from the floor in the far corner. Her sister insisted they each have one in case they needed to follow someone out of town with only a moment's notice. Next, she grabbed a set of keys from the kitchen junk drawer. They belonged to her family cabin in the White Mountains. It would take them three hours to get there. That should be far enough away to keep the four Water Guppies safe. Also, the deed to the cabin was in her mother's maiden name, so it would be more difficult for anyone to find them.

She grabbed an ice chest from the garage and started filling it with water bottles, soda cans, a milk carton, hot dogs, and sandwich meat. Next, she tossed a loaf of bread, hot dog buns, chips, peanut butter, jelly, and a box of cereal into a brown paper bag.

A car horn signaled Meg's arrival out front.

Andi pulled the ice chest out the door, then ran back in for the rest of the food and her Go Bag. She snatched her purse off the kitchen counter on the way outside.

Meg was loading the ice chest into the back of her SUV when Andi stopped to lock her condo door. Andi hurried to catch up and shoved the remaining bags up against the chest. She noticed Meg had also packed her Go Bag. She still had it from the time she had worked for the detective agency as a bookkeeper. It could be a sign she might want to work part-time for them again. The thought made Andi smile.

Andi climbed onto the passenger seat. "Ready?"

"I guess." Meg shifted into drive. "Where to?"

"Ida's. Roxie is hiding everyone there."

Meg's garage door opened, and her son, Chad, backed his older model sedan out onto the driveway.

"I'm glad he hurried as I asked. Okay, insisted." Meg waved at him as he passed, but a concerned expression flickered across her face. "I would have been a mess worrying about him if he hadn't left before me."

Her son waved back and then exited the gate.

Andi's heart ached for her friend. "What did you tell him?"

"That a wicked woman was coming here to hurt Lorraine, so we needed to get her out of town." She turned to face her. "He's been around here long enough to know there are times we need to help keep our friends out of danger."

Andi reached over and patted her friend's arm. "He'll be fine." She could feel the truth of the words as she said them. "Would you rather go with Chad? I would understand if you do."

"He would hate it if I treated him like he was a little kid. Besides, you need help with these spunky grandmas, and if anything does happen, you'll need a nurse."

"True." Andi kept an eye out for Poppy as they drove to the other side of the complex. She also decided to take advantage of the free seconds to call Luke and fill him in on their current situation.

"Wait for me!" He sounded panicked, just as she feared.

"You have jury duty. They'll file a warrant for your arrest if you don't show up."

"I can't sit in a jury box, worrying about you."

Andi knew she would feel the same way if their roles were reversed. "I need you to keep checking the security footage we're getting from the fake bird. Also, if you and

The Cowboy want to put up more cameras, I'll make sure you get reimbursed."

"I'm not concerned about the money. I'm concerned about you."

Meg slowed the SUV, an obvious attempt to give them more time to discuss the matter.

"This is what I need you to do for me," Andi said, knowing Luke had to help or he would defy the court order to appear. "You might record evidence that will put Poppy away, and then I can bring The Water Guppies home. The cabin doesn't have cell service, but I'll sneak into a nearby town in a couple of days to call you."

"In that case, I'll install those cameras today," Luke said. "I want you home as soon as possible. I love you."

"I love you, too." Andi ended the call with a heavy heart. She felt like she had just severed a lifeline.

They found Roxie, Martha, Irene, Lorraine, and a pile of suitcases waiting for them outside Ida's front door. Andi groaned. "I said clothes for a few days, not a year."

"I think the purple case contains Martha's wigs," Meg said with a smile.

"Just what she needs in a forest." Andi jumped out and ran over to help the grandmas carry their bags to the SUV. She ended up securing four suitcases to the roof of the vehicle with bungee cords.

At least they had all dressed in comfortable, pastel-colored jogging suits. It was going to be a long ride. Roxie had attached colorful sequins to her orange suit. She looked like a diva on her way to prison. Andi's stomach clenched at the thought. *I hope that never happens.*

"Where are we going?" Martha asked as she scooted to the far end of the back bench seat.

"A cabin in the woods." Andi turned in her passenger seat up front to catch their reactions to the news.

"Oh, no!" Martha started scooting back out. "I brought the wrong clothes. I need to go home and repack!"

"No, you don't," Andi said. "No one is leaving the cabin once we get there. You can wear your pajamas the whole time if you like."

"Pajamas?" Roxie said. "I forgot mine." Her frown

suddenly faded. "Oh, well, I can sleep in the nude."

"Oh, no, you don't!" Andi pointed to Ida's door. "Go find something to wear to bed. You have one minute."

Irene climbed onto the back bench with Martha as Lorraine climbed onto the seat behind Meg.

"This is all my fault," Lorraine said. "We wouldn't have to hide if I hadn't told everyone about my cousin's idea to invest."

"Are we all going to go to prison?" Irene cupped her cheeks with the palm of her hands. "I'm too old to fight women with skull tattoos."

"Don't worry," Lorraine said. "I'll tell the feds the truth. I told you I had a cousin who could help us invest. You didn't know it was insider trading."

"You did eventually tell us," Martha said.

"Not until after we had already invested, and the police don't need to know that." Tears slid down Lorraine's cheeks.

"Don't cry," Irene said. "We don't want you to go to prison for all of us. We'll figure a way out of this. Won't we, Andi?"

I hope so. "For now, let's just worry about keeping everyone alive," Andi said. "We can worry about the rest later."

****

Andi sat on the passenger side of the SUV, watching the headlights hit upon the dark road and the pine trees in the nearby forest. The confined space smelled like strong perfumes wafting together to create a new CIA torture. For the fourth time in an hour, she pushed the button to open the window and let the cold, clean air inside to sweep the perfume out.

She closed the window and replayed her last meeting with Mack in her mind. *He was sent to Euphoria Lane by the feds. At least that is what he told us. I never actually saw him show any credentials to the police when they arrived after Brad was shot and killed. When Detective Franks arrived, he led Mack away to speak to him in private. None of this proves Mack is a fed. What if he isn't? What if he told me Poppy isn't Brad's cousin because he wanted me to take The Water Guppies away to a location where he can kill them without any witnesses?*

"Turn off your cell phones!" Andi rushed to turn hers off first since Mack had specifically told her to take it along.

Meg took her eyes off the road long enough to send her a disapproving glare. "I need to have mine on in case Chad calls."

"You're not the only one with a son who might call," Roxie said. "I placed several bets that have big payoffs."

Andi held her phone in her hand, wondering what to do next. "Please, do as I say."

Martha harrumphed. "I just want to know why."

"Me, too," Irene said.

"Me, three," Lorraine added.

"Pull over there!" Andi pointed to a dirt area off to the side that was wide enough for them to park safely. She unlocked her seatbelt and shifted in the seat to allow her to speak to everyone and adjust her message according to their reactions. "I don't want to scare anyone."

Meg flipped on the inside light. "No good conversation ever started with those words."

"I'm just trying to be cautious," Andi said. "Mack was the one who thought you were all in danger, and that is why we're headed to the cabin."

"You think he's a bad guy, and we're sitting ducks." Roxie's conclusion was too close for comfort.

Andi met her gaze. "I'm afraid that could be the case if we don't take precautions. The cabin doesn't have cell service, but he could use our phones to track the route we took."

Irene scrambled for her purse. "I'm turning my phone off!"

"Me, too," Lorraine said.

"Me, three," Martha added.

"What about Chad?" Meg looked like she was going to cry.

He did need a way to contact his mother. "Text him my sister's phone number."

"Jessie?"

"Yeah, she's the only one who can help if things get worse." Andi rubbed her forehead. She didn't want him calling Jessie unless it was a true emergency. "Tell Chad that if he needs anything to call Luke, but if he doesn't hear from you in three days to call Jessie and tell her we are staying at the place where our mother fell and lost her tooth."

Irene glanced up from her phone. "Your poor mother!"

Martha gripped her jaw as if it had happened to her.

Roxie laughed. "That must have been funny."

"Roxie!" Lorraine flicked Roxie's beehive hairdo. "You are one wicked woman."

"True." Roxie slapped away Lorraine's hand.

Meg busily typed the message into her phone and then glanced up at Andi. "Should we call your sister and let her know what is going on? She does have a police background."

Andi hated the idea of calling her sister. She needed this vacation with her boyfriend, Derrick, who also worked for their agency. *There has to be a way to make everyone feel safe without bothering Jessie.* A thought came to her.

"Do you trust me?" Andi asked Meg.

"Of course."

Andi turned her phone back on and called the detective in charge of Betsy's murder investigation. When he didn't answer, she left a voicemail. "This is Andi Stevenson. You were speaking to Mack after Brad was shot and killed in front of my condo. Earlier today, Mack told me he is a federal investigator and that Poppy isn't Brad's cousin. He thought I should take Lorraine and her friends away someplace safe. I'm not sure he's telling me the truth. Please look into him. If he's not who he says, please send sheriff's deputies to my family cabin at 4302 West Pine Needle Dr. And please don't tell him where we are even if he is a fed. He might have flipped to the other side of the law. Our lives may depend on you doing as I ask."

When she concluded the call, she shut her phone down—again.

"Do you think Detective Franks even cares about us?"

Lorraine asked. "I got the impression he didn't like you, or maybe it's your sister he doesn't like, and he was taking it out on you."

Andi blew out a quick, short breath. "I'm putting my faith in his reputation, which my sister says is admirable. He's the only one I know who can find out if Mack is legit. Even Jessie doesn't have a connection with the feds."

"I sure hope Mack is a good guy," Irene said. "I wouldn't look good with bullet holes."

"Me, either," the other women said in unison.

Meg smiled when she read aloud the text from her son. "I promise. Mom, be careful. I love you." She typed him back. "I love you, too. I have to shut my phone down now." A tear slid down her cheek as she watched the screen die.

"I'm sorry." Emotion caught in Andi's voice.

"This is all my fault," Lorraine said.

Roxie blew out an exasperated breath. "Lorraine, stop blaming yourself. It isn't helping the situation."

Meg sniffled and wiped away her tears. "Let's get going," she said as she placed both hands on the steering wheel. "It's getting late."

TEN

The SUV's headlights lit up the A-frame cabin where Andi had spent her summers as a child. Her heart warmed before her instincts to protect her friends kicked in. "Circle to the back. We don't want anyone to see your vehicle if they drive by."

"Won't they see the lights in the cabin shining through the windows?" Martha asked.

Roxie unbuckled her seatbelt before they parked. "She's worried about a bad guy driving by and recognizing Meg's car."

Andi opened her door, and the cold air hit her in the face. "I should have thought to remind everyone to bring jackets. I hope we have some inside."

Martha climbed out of the vehicle. "No worries. We always bring sweaters."

"At our age, we're always cold," Irene said.

"Speak for yourselves." Roxie climbed the wooden steps up onto the covered porch.

"Devils are hot creatures." Lorraine chuckled as she joined Andi beside the SUV.

"True." Roxie crossed her arms over her chest. "And yet this old devil is the only one of you over the age of sixty not wanted by the law."

Irene shrugged. "She's got us there."

143

Andi helped Meg pull the suitcases off the roof of the SUV and then carried three up the steps to the back door. She could barely make out the doorknob in the dark.

"Here." Roxie reached her hand into her bra, and after digging around, emerged with a small flashlight. She shined it on the door.

Andi lifted a brow. "What don't you have in there?"

"Are you complaining?"

"No, Ma'am!" Using the circle of light Roxie provided, Andi unlocked the door and pushed it open. The air felt heavy and stale. No one had visited the cabin in over four months.

She reached inside and flipped the lights on. The familiar white appliances and rustic cabinets brought back childhood memories. Andi placed her purse on the long kitchen island where her mother had made their meals every summer. She could almost smell her cherry pie.

The others followed her inside as she made her way to the living room, where she flipped on the overhead fan and lights. The blades spun, kicking up the stale air.

Martha coughed. "Can we open a window?"

"The transom above the door," Andi said. "No one can see us through that window. But we'll need to close it in an hour or so. The temperature will reach freezing later tonight."

Lorraine stepped into the living room with a suitcase in each hand. "Where should we put these?"

The Water Guppies would probably be more comfortable if they didn't have to climb stairs. "There are two rooms with twin beds on this floor." Andi pointed down a long hall. "For safety reasons, we should all share a room with at least one other person. Roxie, you pick the room you and Lorraine want. Irene and Martha will take the other. Meg and I will sleep upstairs."

"Why does Roxie get to pick the room she wants?" Martha whined.

Meg sighed. "Even I know Roxie will end up with the room she wants one way or another."

"Good point," Irene said, following Roxie down the hall. "It's easier this way."

"Give me a minute to turn the water back on, and then you can all freshen up," Andi called after them. "I have to warn you, the water will be cold for awhile. I have to turn on the water heater."

She walked back into the kitchen and pulled open the door, hiding the basement stairs. The darkness and cold always gave her the creeps. She took a step inside and reached up to pull on the thin chain that turned on the overhead lightbulb. Holding onto the railing, she carefully descended the steps until she reached the concrete floor.

Scanning the room, she recognized the washing machine and dryer her mother used daily during their vacations, the extra freezer they filled after each trip to the big warehouse store in the next town, and the aging furnace her father kept swearing he would replace soon. Andi hated this room. It reminded her of every scary movie she had ever watched. The irony that she was now living a scary movie didn't escape her.

She walked over to the old coal chute her grandfather once used and made sure it was locked. The last thing they needed was for someone to sneak inside. After that, she turned the knob that controlled the main water supply to the cabin. They always turned it off when they left to prevent flooding.

After turning on the water heater, she headed back upstairs to the main floor and walked through the cabin. She poked her head into the room Irene and Martha had chosen and found their bedroom window wide open. "You get to choose between the light or the open window. We don't want anyone to see you from the street. It's like placing a target on your back."

"I think we've had enough fresh air." Martha quickly closed the window, locked it, and then pulled the blinds and curtains into place.

When Andi entered Roxie and Lorraine's room, a strong aroma of lavender assaulted her senses. She rubbed her nose.

"I'm getting hungry," Lorraine said.

"I'll cook up the hot dogs I brought with us." Andi stepped back into the hall, away from the lavender oil

Lorraine used like perfume. "Tomorrow we can see what my father left in the freezer."

Roxie dumped her suitcase into a dresser drawer. "Sounds good. I hope he keeps thick steaks in there."

Andi smiled. "He usually does."

When she returned to the living room, she scanned the wooden floor for her Go Bag, but it was no longer there. She climbed the steps to the second floor and found it on the rocking chair in the master bedroom.

Meg was busy neatly unpacking her bag into an empty dresser drawer. "I'll take the first shift keeping guard tonight."

"No, I will," Andi said, while she dumped her bag into a drawer Roxie style. "You drove. You must be exhausted."

At the word exhausted, Meg yawned and then chuckled. "I guess I am."

Andi smiled, then placed her toothbrush and toothpaste in her parents' bathroom. "I'm going to start dinner," she said, before jogging downstairs.

She double-checked to make sure all of the doors were locked and then unpacked the food items she'd brought with her.

The hot dogs were bobbing in a pan of boiling water when Meg entered the kitchen. "I spied out the windows before coming downstairs. Everything looks okay outside. I didn't see or hear anything."

"Thanks." Andi opened the hot dog buns and placed them face down on the hot griddle. "We need to keep checking." A not-so-distant memory came back to her. "My mother saves everything. I bet she still has a baby monitor here."

"Would it work after all these years?" Meg asked incredulously.

Andi laughed. "It wasn't for me. My cousin came up here with her baby last summer, and my mother went overboard on being prepared." She placed a paper plate on the counter. "If you can keep an eye on the buns, I'll be right back."

"Sure, thing." Meg stepped over to the stove.

Andi walked through the living room and found the

four grandmas relaxing on the overstuffed couches, each covered with an afghan. Her mother kept them on the foot of each bed in the cabin. She also noticed the window above the door was closed again and then smiled at the women before heading down the hall to the long row of cabinets. A quick search rewarded her with a baby monitor and her father's stash of batteries. She replaced the old batteries and then carried the two camera units and one parent unit into the kitchen.

"Look what I found." Andi placed her treasures on the island's countertop. "We can hang them where they can show us every side of the house."

Meg furrowed her brow as she removed the toasted hotdog buns from the heat. "You only have two cameras."

"If I attach one to the shed out back, it would be far enough away to pick up the back of the house and the side we drove in on. If I attach the other one to a tree near the road, it can pick up the front and the side with the playhouse."

Meg studied the parent unit, which looked like a small tablet. "Does it have a split-screen?"

"It does. We can view the footage from both cameras at the same time or toggle back and forth. It also has infrared night vision. We'll be able to zoom in to get a good look at anything that comes close to the cabin no matter how dark it gets outside."

"This is a lot better than the one I used with my son," Meg said. "All I usually picked up was static or a boring couple's cell phone call."

"Gotta love modern technology." Andi decided it would be better to eat in the living room instead of gathering The Water Gupppies around a cold table. They looked warm and comfortable beneath the afghans. "If you'll take dinner out to the ladies, I'll hang the cameras outside."

"Deal." Meg grabbed the tongs to remove the hot dogs from the pan of water. "Wear something warm."

Andi grabbed her father's winter coat from the hall closet. The bottom hem reached her knees, and she felt like a little girl playing dress-up in her parent's clothing. After tugging open the back door, she appreciated the extra coverage. The temperature had dropped at least ten degrees since their arrival. The cold immediately seized her face like a mud mask at a spa.

As she traveled across the yard, she held the flashlight in one hand and the camera units in the other. She jumped at every sound and imagined glowing eyes in the surrounding forest as she nestled one unit in the nook of a tree branch where the wind wouldn't carry it away. Next, she removed the protective cover from the adhesive strip on the remaining unit and stuck it to the side of the shed.

When she entered the kitchen, she quickly shut the door and some sense of security settled over her again. She found Meg wolfing down her hot dog at the counter.

Meg lifted her finger for her to wait for a second, swallowed, and then said, "The Water Guppies have their dinner, and I'm going to get some sleep. Wake me in a couple of hours."

"Will do." Andi hung the coat on the back of a dining room chair and then carried her plate and baby monitor into the living room. She set both items down on an end table and then stretched out on her father's leather recliner.

Lorraine sighed. "I didn't mean to cause you all this trouble. If the courts don't take back the money, I'm going to do good and help people with every cent I have left. I'll even give myself community service. There are a lot of places that can use a volunteer."

Irene leaned over and squeezed her hand. "We know you will. You have a big heart. I'll even volunteer with you."

Lorraine wiped away a tear.

Andi took a large bite of her hot dog. She chewed while she studied the split-screen and listened to the grandmas.

Lorraine glanced over at Andi. "I am so sorry. I just wanted to keep up with expenses like my husband and I were able to do before he died. I didn't know we had spent our savings. I'm living Social Security check to Social Security check. At least our home is paid off, but the HOA fee is so high."

"True." Martha placed her empty plate on the oak coffee table. "Can't you do anything about that?"

Andi finished chewing and then swallowed. "I wish I could. The fee covers your water bill as well as the upkeep of the clubhouse, pool, landscaping, outer wall and gate, plus the outside of the buildings, including the rooftops. If you deduct what it would cost if you had to pay for all of that on your own, it's not a bad deal."

"I guess," Martha said. "I would rather pay the HOA for landscaping services than mow my own grass—even if it is only a small patch."

Lorraine rubbed her head. "I should have been happy with my life the way it is. I have a roof over my head and good friends. That's all I really need."

The other Water Guppies agreed.

"We are all fortunate to have good friends," Irene said.

Andi could tell Roxie wanted to make a sarcastic comment but chose to keep her mouth closed. The woman did value her friendship with Lorraine and the other Guppies.

"How did all of this start?" Andi hated to interrupt an emotional moment, but she wanted to know the facts. "Did your cousin mention Brad's insider trading at a family gathering?"

"Heaven's no!" Lorraine waved away the idea. "My cousin, Quin, and I used to place flowers on the graves of our relatives once a month. Afterward, we went to lunch together. During one of these visits, I complained about medical costs. I was having trouble paying for one of my prescriptions. After Medicare chipped in, I was expected to pay six hundred dollars a month."

Roxie huffed. "If you commit a crime because you won't live otherwise, it should be considered self-defense."

Andi knew the woman's heart was in the right place. "I'm sure it would be considered a mitigating factor. At least I hope so."

"Did Quin offer to pay for your meds?" Martha pulled the afghan up closer to her neck.

"Quin? No way!" Lorraine waved that idea as well. "No. He took me into his confidence. He told me about the day he tried to sneak a cigarette behind the investment firm where he worked. Quin was about to light up when he heard someone walk up to the corner—but not all the way to the end where he could see my cousin. Quin immediately recognized Brad's voice. He was talking on the phone to someone who knew about a big company working on a merger with another big company. The information hadn't been made public yet. Brad told the caller he would invest twenty thousand."

"That is what they call insider trading," Irene said. "If you are privy to information that would alter the stock market once it goes public, you cannot invest in that company. Martha Stewart learned the hard way."

Roxie guffawed. "She knew what she was doing."

Lorraine shrugged. "So did I. My cousin told me no one would suspect a little old lady in Arizona of having insider information. I believed him, so I took a chance. I hated to do it, but I sold my late husband's coin collection to purchase the stocks, and I made *a lot* of money. I should have stopped then."

"But you didn't," Andi said.

Lorraine looked sheepishly down at her plate of half-eaten hot dog and chips. "Brad and my cousin must have been taking their breaks at the same time because it happened again. This time, the person on the phone with Brad knew about a defense contractor about to receive a huge government contract. We invested again."

"Your cousin sure knew a lot," Roxie said while chewing her third hot dog. "Did Brad put his phone call on speaker? And are you going to finish your dinner?"

"The speaker wasn't turned on." Lorraine handed her plate to Roxie. "My cousin said Brad asked enough questions for him to figure out what was going on."

"And then she told me about the company getting the government contract," Irene said.

"And me, too," Martha added. "And poor Betsy, God bless her soul."

Roxie narrowed her eyes. "And you left me out of the loop?"

Lorraine lowered her eyes. "I feel really bad about that, but you know you..."

"Have a big mouth," Irene said.

"I'll figure out a way for all of you to make it up to me," Roxie said.

"I'm sure you will." Irene handed Roxie her plate of uneaten chips. "Let's start with this."

Andi wondered if the skinny woman always ate this much or if she had a case of nervous eating like Meg. "Lorraine, getting back to your cousin, why did he bug Brad's office if he could hear him standing outside the building? And why didn't you just sell your husband's coin collection to pay for your medication instead of committing felonies?"

"First, selling my husband's coin collection would only pay for my medications for a year or two. I plan to live a lot longer than that. Second, Quin decided to bug Brad's office after he stopped taking his insider trading calls at the corner of the building, and something happened to make Quin think Brad wasn't covering his tracks as much as he had at first."

Martha leaned closer. "What happened?"

"Well," Lorraine said, "my cousin had just picked up his paycheck one day when he passed by Brad's office and overheard part of a conversation. It sounded like Brad was talking in code and using the same tone of voice he had used outside."

"Tone of voice?" Meg asked as she headed down the stairs earlier than anticipated. She yawned and curled up on an overstuffed chair near the corner.

Lorraine tilted her head and thought for a minute. "You know how you speak to your husband in one tone, your kids in another, your friends in another, and your boss in yet another tone?"

"I get it," Roxie said. "It's like the voice I use to argue with the bartender who always gets my drink order wrong. It's different from the voice I use when my son makes a silly mistake."

"Maybe if you stop telling the bartender he looks like The Unabomber, he might want to get your drink order right," Martha said.

Roxie rolled her eyes. "Maybe if you—"

"Lorraine," Andi interjected before Roxie could say

something biting to Martha. "I assume your cousin discovered more secrets after he planted the bug."

"The first thing he heard was a big chain was going to close hundreds of its stores." Lorraine furrowed her brow. "My cousin handled the investment for me at that time. He called it a short sale. I didn't understand it."

"Join the club," Meg said,

Lorraine glanced at her. "What club?"

Meg shook her head. "Never mind."

"Anyway," Lorraine continued. "The next thing I knew, my cousin said everything was falling apart. He heard Brad telling the person on the phone that he thought someone was on to him. Brad's boss told him that his friend at the SEC was sending an investigator to Arizona to look into a big insider trading case."

They all exchanged a knowing look.

"Mack," Meg whispered.

"Maybe." Andi didn't want to agree with them and make her friend feel worse.

"I look horrible in orange," Lorraine cried. "I don't want to go to jail."

Irene sent her a sympathetic smile. "I'll visit you."

"Me, too," Martha said.

Roxie laughed. "You're both going to jail with her. Thank you for *not* including me in your little club."

"You're so mean." Martha glared at her. "I thought you were Lorraine's friend."

"I am." Roxie shrugged. "But I wasn't the one who got greedy and kept investing. You can get away with investing in one company you have info on if they don't have strong evidence against you. When you use information you're not supposed to have to invest three or four times, it becomes harder to claim it was a coincidence."

"Stop scaring Lorraine, Miss Realist!" Irene demanded.

"Once again, let's get back to the case." Andi chose a potato chip from her plate. "Lorraine, what happened next?"

"You know what happened," she said. "My cousin was afraid Brad might start looking for surveillance equipment since the SEC was possibly onto him, so he snuck into the office to remove the bug and got caught."

Andi pushed a stray lock of hair behind her ear. "And he couldn't tell on Brad because it would implicate him."

Lorraine nodded. "And then Quin thought someone followed him when he came over to my place. He had no clue that he had put my life in jeopardy by coming to see me." Tears welled in her eyes. "He was a good man. I'll miss him. He didn't deserve to die."

"I'm sorry for your loss," Roxie said, surprising everyone with her show of empathy. "He should have carried a gun."

And there was the Roxie they all knew and had grown to love despite her big mouth.

"Speaking of guns," Irene said. "Did anyone bring one?"

"Of course!" Roxie dug into her bra.

"Really?!" Andi hit her forehead with the butt of her hand.

Roxie pulled out the little revolver she called Minnie Pearl.

"What a cute little thing!" Martha cooed. "Do you have tiny candy bullets in there?" She grinned, apparently thinking she'd just put Roxie in her place.

"Let's look." Roxie turned the gun over. A shot rang out, and everyone ducked. A metal ding sounded near the bookshelf. "Whoops!"

Andi walked over to a lampshade and poked her finger through the bullet hole, then she walked over to the bookshelf and searched until she found the bullet embedded into her mother's brass elephant. She turned it around so her mother wouldn't notice the next time she visited the cabin. "Roxie, please leave that thing on the table before you poke someone's eye out."

"Only because I don't want it going off while I'm sleeping and shooting my—"

"We get it," Andi said.

Irene yawned. "I'm getting tired." She stood and draped the afghan over her arm. "I'll see you all in the morning."

"Me, too." Martha stood and stretched before carrying

her afghan down the hall.

Lorraine rubbed her forehead. "I'm getting tired, too, but I don't think I can sleep."

"We can talk until you nod off," Roxie said. She stood and met Andi's gaze. "No, I haven't grown soft."

Andi smiled. "I would never accuse you of being a softie."

"Yeah, right." Roxie walked down the hall with Lorraine.

Meg drew in a deep breath. "You know we shouldn't be here. We should be home, planning your wedding."

"I know." Andi leaned back in the chair and stared at the ceiling. "But I chose to work for my sister's detective agency."

"We would probably be doing this even if you had kept your teaching job."

"You're right," Andi said, picking up the baby monitor and placing it in her lap. "We could never turn our back on The Water Guppies."

"They're grandmas. You can't turn your back on a grandma."

"Especially Lorraine," Andi said.

Meg smiled and nodded. "She looks just like Mrs. Claus."

"She does!" Andi let her head fall back against the chair again and felt her eyes droop.

"You should get some sleep," Meg said. "I'll keep an eye on the monitor."

"Are you sure?" Andi feared what could happen if they both fell asleep.

"Positive." Meg stretched her hand out to receive the monitor. "I feel rested."

"If you're sure."

"I am."

Andi climbed out of her recliner and then walked over to her friend to give her the monitor. "You can see all around the cabin. Look for any movement, and wake me if you see anything out of the ordinary."

"I will, don't worry." Meg grabbed the bag of chips off the coffee table. "I'll need these."

"Your nerves getting to you?"

"Aren't yours?"

Andi pressed her lips together and nodded her acknowledgment. "Their lives are in our hands." She was halfway up the stairs when she turned around. "Wake me in two hours."

Meg lifted her hand to check her watch. "That would be midnight. You got it."

Andi climbed the staircase and headed straight to the bedroom window, where she studied the back of the cabin. With the porch light on, she could see Meg's SUV and the shed her father built while she played with her dolls on the porch. Her gaze traveled to the other side of the yard, where she spotted the firepit where her family roasted marshmallows. She loved this place. She pressed her face closer to the windowpane and stared out into the woods behind the yard. There wasn't any wind, and the stillness felt reassuring. After a few minutes of silence, she kicked off her tennis shoes and then crawled into her parents' bed while still dressed in street clothes—just in case.

****

Andi felt someone shaking her arm. She lifted one eyelid to find Meg hovering above her. "Is it midnight?"

"Shh," Meg warned. "I think someone is outside."

Andi jumped up, now fully alert. "Where?" she whispered.

Meg handed her the baby monitor. "The bushes near the mailbox."

They both peered into the screen, while Andi's eyes tried to adjust to the minimal amount of light in the room.

She held her breath as she watched the wind scatter dead leaves across the front driveway. Suddenly, a raccoon ran out from behind a bush and across the dirt drive. Her heart skipped a beat and then she chuckled with relief. "Thank goodness. This guy has four legs, not two."

Just then, her gaze shifted to the other screen, and she spotted someone wearing a ski mask and dark clothing run from the shed to the back porch.

155

Meg grabbed hold of her arm. "Did you see that?"

"I'm going to get Roxie's gun." Andi pulled her arm out of Meg's grip. "Wake the grandmas and tell them to be quiet."

"Should we call the sheriff's department?"

"Remember, we don't get cell phone service here." Andi slipped on her tennis shoes. "My parents don't have a landline either."

Meg huffed. "Why did we choose a hiding place without a landline?"

"Because it's the only decent place to stay that doesn't require we show identification or a credit card."

"True." Meg frowned and then took off to wake The Water Guppies.

Andi held onto the small monitor as she ran down the steps. The masked man tried to peer through the window blinds at the back of the cabin. Andi skipped the bottom step as she jumped onto the main floor and snatched the gun off the end table where Roxie had left it.

The cold metal felt foreign in her hands. While holding it tight with one hand, she stared down at the baby monitor. The masked man tried to turn the knob on the locked back door. He or she dug into pockets and pulled out some type of card.

Andi's breath caught in her throat. The wind whistling through the cabin added to the scariness factor of the moment and sent shivers down her spine.

She held out the gun—ready to shoot—while walking quickly to the kitchen. *The second that door opens, I'm shooting.*

Meg appeared behind her. The Water Guppies, minus Roxie, huddled behind the table. They looked defenseless in their bathrobes and slippers. Andi held up the monitor for Meg to see but kept it close so the light wouldn't shine through the drapes and blinds in the windows. Meg gripped Andi's arm so hard she could feel her friend's nails digging into her skin.

A scraping sound signaled the masked man was trying to open the door by pushing the card between the door frame and lock. Andi had tried that method before and only succeeded with cheap bedroom locks. Luckily, her father had made sure they didn't have cheap locks.

"The baseball bat is in the closet beside the front door," Andi whispered.

"I'll be right back." Meg finally released her grip on Andi's arm and slipped away.

Roxie entered the kitchen, wearing baggy white PJ loungewear with huge red hearts all over. It must have been the only outfit she could find in Ida's drawers before they had left town. With a look of determination on her face, she snuck over to the dish strainer and grabbed the hot dog pan. "Let's trade," she whispered to Andi.

Andi shook her head, unable to get over how pale Roxie looked without her makeup even in the darkened room.

"It's my gun. I'll shoot, and then you knock him unconscious so he can't shoot back."

That actually makes sense. "Wait until he gets inside before you shoot," Andi said as she handed over the gun.

"Why?"

"I can't knock him out if I can't see him," Andi said. "Besides, if he dies, we'll have a stronger self-defense case."

Roxie shrugged. "Have it your way."

The knob jiggled, and a whispered chorus of female gasps filled the room. When the door refused to open, they released their pent up breath.

Andi played with the pot in her hand, trying to determine if it could knock someone out. She handed it back to Irene and then opened a cupboard to retrieve her mother's cast-iron skillet. When she turned around, she spotted Lorraine holding her knitting needles like knives, and Martha holding a fire poker like a sword. She wondered if she should warn their trespasser that they were armed but decided against it. He might come back with a hand grenade—or worse.

"I've never killed anyone before," Martha whispered. "Do we all jump on him at once, or do we take turns?"

Roxie sighed. "You three stand back around the corner."

Meg returned with the bat. "If he gets past us, let Irene hit him over the head with the pot, then Martha should stab him with the poker, and then Lorraine can follow up with the needles."

"Or you can hide in the basement?" Andi suggested. "My mother has a big pantry down there."

They looked at one another and nodded like bobblehead dolls. Andi quietly snatched the flashlight from under the sink and then pointed to the door next to the refrigerator. They filed out one after the other. That left Meg, Roxie, and Andi to fight the battle—if there was one.

Andi stared into the monitor she held in one hand while holding the skillet in the other. The man in the mask moved away from the door and walked to the window above the kitchen sink. Andi dropped to her bottom on the wooden floor and leaned against the cabinet. She pressed the monitor against her chest to keep the light from giving away her location.

Meg dropped to her knees, holding the bat tight as she leaned against a cabinet as well. Roxie held onto the counter and lowered to her knees, then shuffled backward out of sight.

That's a good idea. Andi scooted away from the window on her bottom, still pressing the monitor against her chest and holding onto the skillet. Meg and Roxie shuffled on their knees until all three of them gathered under the kitchen table.

The window wobbled in its track, and Andi's heart jumped.

Meg held the bat in front of her face. "What's the plan?"

"If he pokes his head inside, I'll shoot," Roxie whispered.

"When he falls inside, I'll rush forward and hit him on the head," Andi said. "And then you hit him on the other side of his head."

Andi snuck a peek at the masked man's movements through the monitor. He grabbed a milk crate from under a chair on the porch and placed it in front of the window.

"Here we go," Andi said, watching him step up onto the crate. She placed the monitor face down on a chair cushion. "Stick to the plan."

The window rattled again, partly from the wind but

mostly from his efforts, until the lock on the bottom fell away.

"I'm too young to die," Meg whispered.

The window scraped against the metal track as he forced it to move to the side.

Andi's breathing turned shallow as she froze in place.

Meg grabbed onto Andi's arm.

A gloved hand reached inside the darkened room through the opened window to pull up the blinds and push aside the cheery yellow drapes. If they had been asleep, the sounds would have wakened them but not soon enough to stop him.

Andi pressed her lips together.

Don't scream. You can handle this. You've done it before.

He held onto the bottom of the window frame as he poked his head inside. The whites of his eyes shined through the holes in the mask.

Please don't see us in the dark.

Without saying a word, he pushed the top half of his body up through the open window like a mermaid emerging from the ocean.

Roxie reached her hand out from under the table and fired.

Andi shuddered. Meg buried her head in Andi's back.

The sound of metal signaled the bullet most likely missed its target and hit the sink instead.

Andi heard the masked man mutter something. The sound was low and guttural. It sounded like it came from a man, but she couldn't swear to it. She also didn't recognize the voice.

He—or she—ducked and struggled to back out to freedom.

Meg and Andi jumped out from under the table and rushed forward.

Meg swung the bat, striking the masked intruder's shoulders. That wasn't the plan, but that was okay. She did what she could.

Andi pictured the defenseless grandmas in her care and knew she had to stop this possible murderer. She swung the skillet as the intruder was almost completely out of the window. The skillet hit both the window frame and his skull. A thud sounded throughout the room, and Andi's wrist felt a striking pain. She took control of the skillet with her good hand—just in case she needed to strike again.

The possible killer groaned and slipped back onto the wooden porch. A louder thud sounded outside. Most likely from him landing on the wooden planks below.

Lights from a car pulling up to the front of the cabin lit up the living room and the far end of the kitchen.

Roxie lifted her gun. "He might have a partner!"

They all ran to the sides of the front window. Andi peeked through the blinds, and her wrist ached with each movement. She resisted the urge to check for a possible sprain—for now.

Meg flipped on the front floodlights, revealing a man they knew. He stood next to a sedan parked on the driveway, shielding his eyes from the sudden bright light.

"It's Detective Franks!" Andi ran to unlock the front door. She spotted Roxie escaping to the kitchen. *Maybe she's afraid he'll arrest her.*

The second the door stood open, Meg ran out into the arms of the detective. "Help! Someone tried to kill us."

He pried her off his body and then glanced over at Andi with a questioning expression on his tired-looking face.

"Someone tried to break in through the kitchen window," she said, letting the skillet dangle at her side.

Roxie rushed back into the living room. "He's gone!"

Andi furrowed her brow. "Who's gone?"

"The guy!" She dramatically pointed toward the back of the house. "I just went out there to check on him. He's gone!"

"Stay inside." The detective removed his gun from its holster. "All of you," he said directly to Andi. "And lock the doors." With his gun ready, he walked around the outside of the cabin.

Andi turned and caught Roxie slipping her gun behind the throw pillow she sat next to on the couch. "What are you doing?"

Roxie lifted her finger to her thin lips until Meg entered

the cabin and locked the door. "Minnie Pearl isn't registered," Roxie said.

Andi rolled her eyes and released an exasperated breath. She knew she'd asked Roxie months ago if she had registered the gun. The woman had lied to her and not for the first time. She wasn't going to get into it with her as long as the detective remained on the premises, but she would—later.

"The Water Guppies," Meg said. "They're still downstairs.

"I'll make sure they're okay." Andi set the skillet down on the dining room table and then pulled open the basement door using both hands. The area below the stairs was pitch black. Since the detective was on the property, she figured it was safe to pull the chain to turn on the single bulb hanging above. She carefully descended the stairs and then flipped on the light switch on the wall.

Meg slowly made her way down the stairs, gripping the wooden rail and moving her head back and forth like a searchlight to scan the area.

Andi felt a cold breeze in the room before she spotted the opened coal chute. Her first thought was the masked man. The same person who had killed Brad might have managed to break open the chute. She raced to the walk-in pantry door and tugged it open. She found a multitude of shelves stocked with canned goods and water bottles but no grandmothers. Andi lifted Martha's red bathrobe off the concrete floor. *They must have used it to sit on.*

Roxie appeared at the top of the stairs. "What's taking so long?"

"Where are they?" Fear gripped Meg's words.

"I don't know!" Andi gripped the bathrobe closer and took in the scent of Martha's lavender oil. "I told them to hide in here."

"He took them!" Meg ran her hand through her blonde hair. "It's our fault. We should have told them to hide in your parent's bedroom upstairs where they would have been safe."

"We didn't know what would happen." Andi patted Meg's shoulder. "Try to stay calm," she said, before rushing back upstairs to find Detective Franks.

At that moment, he entered the cabin through the back door, which Roxie must have left unlocked. "I didn't see your intruder out there, but I did find a milk crate under the kitchen window. I assume he stood on it to break in."

"I could have told you that," Roxie said, patting her beehive hairdo that had remained intact despite the events of the evening.

"Never mind that now," Andi said. "We're missing three of our friends. They were hiding in the basement."

"You mean the three women I found hiding in the SUV?" He turned and ushered in the grandmas. Black soot covered their bodies and bathrobes from head to foot.

Irene touched her cheek, and her movements spread soot down to her chin. "We heard the ruckus upstairs and got scared. We left the pantry to try to figure out what was going on and what we should do."

"We could see out through the window down there." Martha pulled her soiled white robe tighter around her thin body. "The guy in the ski mask took off into the woods."

"We were afraid he might come back," Lorraine said. In her red pajamas covered with soot, she looked like she'd followed Santa down the chimney. "We crawled out the coal chute to get to the SUV before he had a chance to return."

Roxie planted her hands on her bony hips and glared at her friends.

Irene's jaw dropped open. "I swear we were going to send someone to knock on the door and collect you all as soon as we got the car started."

"I certainly hope so," Roxie griped.

"But then we realized hotwiring a car looks easier on TV than it is in reality," Martha said.

Roxie groaned. "It never dawned on you that I could hotwire a car?"

"I have the keys." Meg removed a set of keys from her pocket and dangled them for all to see. "You could have come upstairs to get us instead of going out through the chute."

"We realized that *after* we couldn't get the car started." Irene shrugged, looking sheepishly at both Meg and Andi.

"We were going to come to get you, but..." Martha said. "We heard another ruckus coming from the front of the cabin."

"That was my arrival," the detective said.

"We didn't know that at the time." Lorraine noticed the red fabric in Andi's hand and reached for her bathrobe.

"We were afraid the masked guy was back," Irene said. "So we hid in the SUV."

"And I found you," the detective said.

"Thanks for letting us know we were safe now." Martha unclutched her hands and then rubbed at the soot on her fingers. "Is it okay for us to take showers and clean up now?" She looked like a puppy, waiting for approval.

"Go ahead," the detective said. "I'll be here for a while. Just make sure you see me before I leave. I want to ask you a few questions."

The three Water Guppies promised and then retreated to their rooms.

"I am so glad you're here," Meg told the detective as she crossed her arms over her chest.

Andi noticed he looked haggard. "Why are *you* here?"

"You did leave me a message," he said, rubbing his jaw with the pad of his thumb. "And you weren't answering your cell phone."

"We don't get cell service here," Andi said. "I was hoping you might try to call and send a sheriff's deputy by to check on us. I didn't expect you to make the trip yourself."

"Calling the sheriff's office did cross my mind," he admitted. "But then I made a call to a friend of mine in Washington, D.C."

"Oh?" Andi raised a brow. "What did you find out?"

"Mr. Young is with the SEC."

"Who?" Meg asked.

"Mack," Andi said, fearing how her friend might take the answer.

Meg raised her voice. "He's what?!"

"A retired investigator with the Securities and

Exchange Commission." Detective Franks turned back to Andi. "After I asked about him, I received a call from his supervisor. He said Mack served admirably for over thirty years and was asked to come out of retirement for six months, but they haven't been able to get in touch with him for over twenty-four hours."

"I spoke to him earlier today," Andi said, glancing at Meg to make sure she was still okay. "He told me to take the ladies out of town, but I got a strange feeling about it on the way up here."

Franks examined the window where the masked man broke in as he spoke. "All I know is he isn't returning calls to his superiors," Franks said. "I'm not sure what that means for all of you."

"Me, either," Andi said. *Is Mack one of the bad guys? Did he try to break in? Or was it Poppy?*

Agitated, Meg ran her hand through her hair. "What do we do now? We can't go home, and we can't stay here."

Roxie pulled a chair out from the kitchen table and sat down. "I have an idea."

****

Andi sat at her dining room table, typing an email to the group taking baking lessons at the clubhouse. "We will be meeting again tonight at seven o'clock. Sorry for the last-minute notice. Hope to see you all there."

"Sounds good," Meg said on a yawn. "I am so glad we took a day to rest before coming back here."

"Me, too." The time off had given Andi's hand a chance to heal. It turned out she hadn't sprained it when she swung the cast-iron skillet at the masked man and hit both him and the window frame. The Water Guppies applied heat, cold, creams, and over-the-counter meds to get her back to normal in no time. Andi drew the line at Roxie's acupuncture needles. At least she didn't keep those in her bra.

Before leaving the cabin, they had all agreed they couldn't implement Roxie's plan because she wanted to storm Poppy and Mack's condos with machine guns. They also agreed they couldn't come up with a new plan unless they slept first. Andi knew where her sister's boyfriend, Derrick, kept a spare key to his house. He had gone out of town with her sister, Jessie, so none of the new neighbors had a chance to meet him. They didn't know he was a former police officer, he worked for Jessie's detective agency, and his house contained enough guns and ammo to hold off a small army. Andi had also brought the baby monitoring system back with them and installed it in Derrick's yard.

Luke had rushed straight over to Derrick's house after jury duty. He kept guard over them while they slept, which was the only reason Andi could relax. She slept close to him on the couch while he watched the perimeter on the monitor. Later, he had agreed to stay there with the Water Guppies while Meg, Roxie, and Andi returned to Euphoria Lane. He didn't like staying behind, but he knew Andi needed him there.

Andi pushed the button to send the email regarding the baking class and then turned to her friend. "Are you ready?"

"As ready as I'll ever be." Meg picked up the grocery bag containing flour, sugar, and eggs. "I hope your plan for tonight works."

"Me, too," Andi said. Luke had placed additional cameras around the Euphoria condominium complex while they were at the cabin, but none in the clubhouse and none recording Poppy doing anything illegal. Andi grabbed her tote bag containing the hidden cameras they'd bought on their way to Derrick's house.

Meg opened the front door. "What are we going to do if we see Poppy or Mack? We still don't know which one tried to break into the cabin."

"Pretend we don't suspect anything. That's all we can do unless one of them tries to harm us."

"Then, we use your sister's stun gun?"

Andi patted the holster hidden beneath her flowing blouse. "Immediately!"

After locking up, they walked at a brisk pace down the road that circled the complex. They also glanced in every direction to make sure no one followed them. Meg stood guard behind Andi as she unlocked the door. Before entering, they heard the familiar hum of a motor.

"Wait for me!" Roxie yelled as she rode up on The Cowboy's golf cart.

"What is she doing here?" Andi asked, standing next to the door. "I thought she was going to watch Poppy's condo from The Cowboy's window."

"Why are you asking me? I've been with you the whole time." Meg didn't wait for the golf cart to park. She carried a brown paper sack inside.

Andi waited for Roxie to catch up. Instead of her usual bright jumpsuits, she wore a solid black one. She had also replaced her stilettos with black tennis shoes. "That's a new style for you."

"After what happened at the cabin, I want to be ready to run at a moment's notice." She turned to The Cowboy, who remained seated in the golf cart. "Are you coming in?"

"Nope." He drove the cart onto the grass and then backed it up against the clubhouse's garage door. "I'm going to keep watch out here."

Roxie waved and then sashayed inside on her tennis shoes.

Andi closed the door. "Why aren't you spying on Poppy's condo?"

"She's not there." Roxie took the eggs Meg had unpacked and placed them inside the refrigerator. "Get this! Her place is empty."

"What do you mean it's empty?" Meg unlocked the pantry, which held the rest of the baking supplies.

"*Empty* as in The Cowboy and I looked through Poppy's window and her furniture is gone!" Roxie threw her hands up in the air. "She moved out!"

"She may have moved her stuff out," Andi said, "but that does not mean we are all safe if she's the one who shot Brad."

"It could mean she took off to hide." Meg carried mixing bowls to the kitchen island for that evening's baking class.

Roxie climbed onto a stool at the kitchen island.

Andi leaned against the counter. "She might be planning for a quick getaway after she shoots us. We need to be prepared just in case she shows up here. I have the taser, but you will both need something."

"Roxie can beat her with a rolling pin," Meg said as she broke into a fit of laughter.

"I get it," Roxie said. "You heard the rumor *I started* about breaking someone's knees with a rolling pin. You laugh now, but that rumor got a lot of tough guys to pay their gambling debts to my son." Roxie removed her pistol from her bra. "Besides, I don't need a rolling pin. I still have Minnie Pearl."

Andi rolled her eyes. "I told you to hide Minnie until you get her registered."

"I'm in *the process* of registering her."

"Yeah, right." Andi huffed while she walked over to the table to start unpacking her tote bag.

"Is your son still a bookie?" Meg asked in an obvious attempt to change the subject.

"He's a very good one," Roxie said. "But now that his son is a little older, Buddy is thinking of moving to Nevada, where he can use his talents to find a legit job."

Meg frowned. "He's going to take your grandson away from you?"

Roxie waved away the notion. "I know my son. He'll send Bobby to me every time he has a break from school."

Meg smiled. "That will be fun for you."

"I'll remember you said that when I need a sitter."

Meg's eyes widened. "I didn't—"

"Sure, you did." Roxie slid off the stool and walked over to Andi. "What are those?"

"Hidden cameras." Andi lifted a clock in the shape of a black cube. "We're going to place this on the bookshelf in the living room, facing the kitchen. I want to record anyone who comes in here."

"And this?" Roxie lifted a silver radio. "I didn't know people used radios anymore."

"Which is why it will fit into a community clubhouse—a place where you would expect to find old things. It also happens to contain another hidden camera." Andi placed the radio on a kitchen counter and turned it to face an area not captured by the clock cube.

Roxie picked up a stuffed toy reindeer with a red bow tied around its neck. She flipped it over and pulled the price tag off. "Does this have a hidden camera, too?"

Meg smiled at Andi.

"Not yet," Andi said.

Roxie tossed the toy up in the air. "What do you hope to catch with the cameras?"

Andi caught the toy and then ran her finger over its glowing nose. "We sent out an email to the baking class attendees, telling them we rescheduled the baking lesson for tonight. Both Mack and Poppy will receive the message."

Meg placed measuring spoons in front of the mixing bowls. "We're hoping that the real killer will take advantage of the class to try to kill The Water Guppies."

"Aren't we going to be in the room when this goes down?" Roxie asked. "Isn't that a tad bit dangerous?"

"Only a little," Andi said. "Detective Franks will be here in a few hours, and he'll have men placed all over the property before anyone arrives for the class."

Roxie rolled her eyes. "Are they going to let Mack and Poppy inside the clubhouse? You should have let me buy machine guns."

Meg frowned, and Andi lost confidence in her plan. *Should I call this whole thing off?*

"Roxie, you don't have to be here," Andi said. "And maybe you should stay home, too," she told Meg.

"No way!" Roxie patted her beehive hairdo. "I'm not afraid."

"I'm afraid," Meg said, "but I want this to be over, and Andi's plan is the best way to lure the killer out into the open. Besides, if Detective Franks thought this was too dangerous, he wouldn't let us do it."

"Keep telling yourself that," Roxie said as she tapped her fingernails on the tabletop.

Andi handed a camera and the reindeer to Meg, then opened the blinds in the window and said, "Let's get this place set up, and then we can leave the rest up to the professionals. Detective Franks will stop anyone approaching the clubhouse."

"That makes sense," Meg said. "I can live with that plan."

Roxie guffawed. "You hope!"

Meg narrowed her eyes. "You mean, *we* hope. You're going to be here, too. Right?"

"Right." Roxie rolled her eyes and then watched Meg hide the camera inside of the toy reindeer. "Wow! You're good at that. I might need to call on you one day."

"I work for pumpkin spice lattes," Meg said. "Are we ready?" she asked Andi.

"In one second." Andi placed the reindeer on a bookshelf where it would record anyone approaching the sliding glass door. "We're heading back to my place to watch the camera footage," she told Roxie. "Do you want to join us?"

"Nope." She placed her hand on her hip. "I'm going to take advantage of this alone time with The Cowboy to win him over with my womanly charms."

Meg coughed.

Andi waggled her eyebrows suggestively. "Have fun."

They watched Roxie dance out the door and then exchanged knowing smiles.

"If he hadn't dealt with large, unpredictable cattle most of his life," Meg said, "I'd be worried about him."

"If anyone can handle Roxie, it's a rancher—or a mafia hitman." Andi locked up and then waved to the couple in the golf cart. She heard Roxie tell The Cowboy they were supposed to drive around the property to hunt down Poppy and Mack. Andi cleared her throat but not loud enough to attract his attention. *Perhaps an armed police officer should ride along with them.*

Meg fell into step beside her as they walked down the road. "Do you think the man in the mask was Mack?"

"I'm not even positive it was a man. It could have been Poppy, but then it could have been Mack. I don't know." Andi glanced over at her friend and noticed the pain behind her eyes. "I'm sorry he lied to you."

"Not as sorry as I am." They stepped off the asphalt of

the road and onto the sidewalk in front of Andi's condo. "I was enjoying the giddy feeling I got whenever I saw him. I felt like a teenager again. Know what I mean?"

"I know what you mean." Andi smiled at how she still got excited whenever Luke called her or showed up at her door. She wished their lives would return to normal so she could spend the evening alone with him. She missed him.

Andi unlocked her condo door and headed straight to the dining room table, where she had left her laptop. She stopped short when she noticed it stood open. "I know I shut this down before we left."

Meg's eyes widened. "I know you did, too." She nervously glanced to the left into the kitchen and then to the right into the living room. "I watched you do it.

Andi removed the stun gun from the holster at her waist. "Stay behind me."

"We should call the police." Meg removed her cell phone from her pocket. "I'm going to call the detective. I put his number into my contacts."

"Then stand by the door while I check the front rooms." Andi listened to Meg's soft voice behind her as she summoned the courage to open the coat closet. She placed her free hand on the doorknob. *Three, two, one!*

She yanked open the door.

Coats. She glanced down at the carpet—a *coat on the floor.*

She drew in a deep breath and then walked over to the sofa and glanced behind it—*dusty carpet.*

Next, she walked over to the bathroom. She breathed in deeply and then quickly glanced inside at the shower—a *shampoo container. I need more conditioner.*

Andi headed to her sister's room. The door stood open, and she tiptoed inside. Jessie had left her bed unmade. She stepped closer to the bed and forced herself to look underneath. *Shoe boxes. Too many shoeboxes.*

Next, she stood to the side and pushed open the closet's sliding door—*clothes and more shoes.*

The inspection of her own bedroom came up with the same results—only fewer shoes. On the way back to the dining room, she noticed her opened desk drawer in the living room. *Someone went through my desk!*

Upon further inspection, she discovered someone had gone through the notebook she'd left on top of her desk. She could tell because the page where she had recently scribbled down phone numbers was missing. Someone had ripped it out.

Meg walked up behind her. "The detective is sending a squad car."

"I think someone broke in to find out where The Water Guppies are hiding." Andi waved the notebook in the air. "That's the only reason I can think of that someone would go through my desk and check my laptop. Fortunately, they wouldn't have found The Water Guppies that way."

Meg removed her phone from her pocket. "I'm going to let the detective know."

Andi pushed the button to turn on her laptop and then entered her password. As she eased into the chair, she navigated to the website that would show her the security footage from the front gate and the clubhouse.

The clubhouse kitchen appeared on the screen first. The baking stations were prepared for the evening's class just as they had left them. Andi moved the computer mouse around and created a split-screen with four sections. She could see the front gate, the clubhouse kitchen, its main room, and the view through its sliding glass door.

"Detective Franks is on his way over," Meg said as she joined Andi at the table. She eased onto a chair and sighed. "I am so ready for all of this to be over."

"I'm afraid that thought will have to wait," Andi said, leaning closer to the screen. She pointed to the guy at the clubhouse's sliding glass door.

"No way!" Meg leaned over to look closer at the screen. "Who is that?"

A young guy, maybe nineteen or twenty, wore jeans and a T-shirt with a skull logo. He managed to open the sliding glass door without much effort and then entered the room. After a quick look around, he crept into the kitchen. He removed a small baggie with a powder in it and began sprinkling it inside of the flour containers in the three stations. He sealed the bag up and shoved it into his pocket. He then glanced down at his watch before quickly removing a spoon from a drawer and using it to mix the powder into the flour at each station.

"I'm betting that's rat poison!" Meg said, reaching into her pocket for her cell phone. "We have to make sure no one uses that flour! I'll text Roxie."

"I've never seen that guy before," Andi said, watching Meg text Roxie. "Do you know who he is?"

"He looks like the kind of thug you hire when you want to get a job done."

Andi watched him drop the spoon into the dishwasher and then sneak back out the sliding glass door. She turned to face Meg. "The killer is getting rid of witnesses. I'm guessing that kid will go back to whoever hired him to kill us. He'll expect to get paid, and then no one will ever see him alive again."

"What do we do?" Meg asked. "We don't know who hired him, and we won't know where to send the police once they get here."

Andi knew what she needed to do. "I'm going to follow him."

"Not without me!" Meg beat her to the door.

ELEVEN

Andi and Meg ran out of the condo without taking time to lock up.

"There he is!" Meg kept her voice low and pointed to the thug walking quickly across the road in front of the clubhouse toward the entrance to the complex. They stood two buildings away to his right. If he scanned the area around him, he might see them.

"Follow me." Andi crept forward between garage doors and the front of vehicles parked in driveways. Up ahead, a car drove onto the property, and the thug walked out through the opened gate. Once he was no longer in their line of vision, they both ran in his direction.

When they reached the end of the last building, Andi poked her head out far enough to spot the thug turning onto a sidewalk that ran alongside a residential street. The large gate finished closing before they could follow him.

Andi rushed forward.

"Here!" Meg tossed Andi her key to the side gate for people walking in and out of the complex.

Andi reached the gate first, inserted the key into the lock and twisted. She pulled it open and waited for Meg to hurry through the exit. She then tossed the key back to Meg and joined her at the end of the property line, where the outer wall curved near the street. They poked their heads out far enough to spot him walking down the sidewalk toward the next corner.

"Let's stick close to the wall." Andi crept to the first set of tall bushes, and when she felt it was safe, she rushed to the next. Meg followed her lead.

Once the thug turned the next corner where two residential streets intersected, they ran on the grass next to the sidewalk to limit the amount of noise they made. When they neared the corner, they slowed their pace.

Upon reaching the end of the wall, they poked their heads out again. Luckily, a bush provided some cover. They watched the thug cross the street and then continue walking down the sidewalk. He suddenly turned, and they jerked back quickly.

"Do you think he saw us?" Meg asked.

"We'll find out in a second." Andi placed her phone on record and then flattened her body on the grass. She held the phone up enough to reach an opening in the bush that would allow her to record his movements across the street. After thirty seconds, which seemed like an eternity, she pulled the phone down. They leaned against the wall, hidden from his line of vision, and viewed the film footage.

The thug had continued walking briskly, looking forward, and not around him.

"He isn't worried about someone following him," Meg surmised.

"To be on the safe side," Andi said, "let's stick to the bushes and cars."

They continued to follow him without being noticed. Soon, he reached a small community park. They crouched down to hide behind the front of a white sedan parked along the curb.

Andi checked her watch. *Five o'clock. Families are home for dinner.*

Her stomach growled at the thought.

"Shh," Meg whispered.

"Not my fault."

"Sorry."

They watched in silence as the thug walked over the abandoned basketball court toward a copse of trees. He suddenly stopped and removed a pack of cigarettes from his pocket. He lit a cigarette with a lighter.

"You think he's waiting for someone?" Meg asked.

"Maybe," came a male voice behind them. "Who are you spying on?"

Andi jolted. She turned to find Mack squatting on the asphalt beside them. "Why should we tell you?"

Meg narrowed her eyes. "You might be a bad guy."

"If I'm the bad guy, why is Poppy walking straight for the only person in the park you could be spying on?"

"What?" Andi turned and spotted Poppy's red hair gently bobbing up and down on her shoulders as she walked casually toward the thug. She looked like any of the other neighbors in her jeans and dark sweatshirt. Only they knew she wasn't just another neighbor. *She must have hired him to poison our baking supplies.* While Poppy talked to the guy, she kept glancing around them. Andi flattened her body so she could watch from under the car. The others copied her with Mack sticking close to Meg.

"What are we watching?" Mack said.

"We caught that guy doctoring our baking flour," Andi said.

He glanced over at her. "He's trying to kill you?"

"We think Poppy wants to *kill all of us*," Meg said. She removed her cell phone from her pocket and began recording the scene.

They all watched Poppy remove a wad of cash from her pocket and hand it over to the thug. Andi couldn't make out his expression exactly, but it looked like a grin. Poppy stepped closer to the thug, and a moment later, he fell to the grass.

"Oh, no!" Meg yelled.

Poppy looked in their direction, took two steps backward, and then started running away.

Mack ran after her.

Meg jumped up and called 9-1-1 as she rushed towards the thug.

Andi wanted to stay and help Meg, but she still wasn't sure whose side Mack was on. "I'll be back," she told her friend and then took off after the others.

Poppy ran between two houses, across a street, between two other houses, and then sprinted across a golf course. She glanced back at Mack, who kept gaining ground, and she almost ran into a golf cart. She weaved at the last moment. The man driving pressed down on the horn and yelled at her.

Andi managed to keep pace but was unable to run fast enough to close the gap. *I'm out of shape!*

Poppy reached the opposite side of the golf course and ran between two more houses. Mack followed close behind, while Andi followed Mack. She lost sight of Poppy when she turned behind a house up ahead. Then she lost sight of Mack.

Reaching the same corner, she spotted Mack jumping over someone's back yard wall. She ran to the same wall and was about to jump up and grab hold of the top when she heard Mack. "Poppy! Stop! You're under arrest!"

Andi followed the wall around to a gate and peered through the opening where the wood panel hung on hinges. She could only make out the side of Mack's body. A shot rang out, and he jerked backward before falling face forward to the ground.

She shuddered. *No!*

Her pulse skipped a beat when she heard what she presumed was Poppy running in her direction, straight toward the gate. Andi stepped around the corner where she couldn't be seen and removed the stun gun from its holster. Her heart pounded in her chest as she listened to Poppy flip up the latch and then push the wooden gate open.

Andi wasn't sure if she should lunge forward and risk getting caught or wait to see if Poppy turned the corner and spotted her, which would risk getting shot.

Poppy exited the gate and started toward the driveway, away from Andi. She knew she couldn't let her escape, especially if she might have just killed a federal investigator.

Andi removed the safety from the stun gun and then picked up a rock and threw it at the large trash can in front of Poppy to distract her. While the woman investigated the noise, Andi drew in a deep breath and ran straight toward her.

Poppy spun around, and her eyes widened in surprise. Andi jumped on top of her, forcing them both to the ground. She pressed the electrodes against Poppy's neck and pulled the trigger. Poppy jerked violently, and Andi struggled to keep the stun gun against her body for more than a second or two.

When Poppy passed out, Andi removed the gun and checked for signs of breathing. She spotted the other woman's chest moving, and relief swam over her. She was still alive.

Andi drew in a deep breath and pushed herself awkwardly up to her feet. *Mack!*

She slipped into the back yard and found him trying to walk toward her. His hand covered a bloody area on his pale blue shirt.

"Are you all right?" She ran over to help.

"Really?" he said. "I've been shot."

"At least you're not dead." She wrapped his arm around her shoulder and helped him walk over to a lawn chair. "By any chance, do you have handcuffs?"

He closed his eyes and nodded, then leaned to the side and removed a set from his back pocket. "Did you catch her?"

"Me and my sister's stun gun."

He smiled as he handed the metal bracelets over to her.

She rushed back to Poppy's prone body, not sure how long she would remain unconscious. She pulled both hands behind her back and secured the cuffs. "Now, you're under arrest."

With that done, she removed her cell phone from her pocket and called 9-1-1.

****

Andi sighed. She was beginning to hate hospital waiting rooms; all she did there was wait and worry.

Meg sat next to her, checking her watch for the twelfth time in ten minutes. "I wish those investigators would leave Mack's room so I can go in."

Andi pressed her lips together. "What are you going to say?"

"I don't know. Part of me wants to tear into him, and part of me wants to thank him for chasing Poppy. If he hadn't taken that bullet, Poppy might have shot you."

Andi lifted a brow. "That wouldn't have been a good thing."

"True." Meg smiled at her. "Since Mack's recovering from yesterday's surgery, I guess I shouldn't be too hard on him."

Thirty minutes later, two men in suits stepped out of Mack's room and walked to the elevator. When the doors closed and they disappeared from view, Meg slowly stood.

Andi glanced up at her. "Do you want me to go in with you, or do you want me to stay here and wait?"

She mulled it over for a moment. "Can you stand at the door? Knowing you are close will give me the moral support I need to confront him."

"Anything you need. I'm here for you."

Together, they walked down the hall. Andi sent her friend a warm smile before pushing open the door to his room. The aroma of rubbing alcohol and his half-eaten lunch blended in the air.

Andi spotted Mack resting in his bed, staring at a blank television screen. His pale complexion worried her, but Meg looked at the vitals displayed on the monitors and didn't appear upset.

"Interesting TV show?" Meg asked as she stepped to his bedside.

"Very." He glanced up at her with a puzzled expression and then pressed the button in the remote to lift the top half of his bed into a sitting position. "I didn't expect to see you here."

"I didn't expect to be here." Meg glanced back at Andi, who gave her a thumbs-up sign. Meg nodded as she appeared to summon the courage to continue. "I now know you're not one of the bad guys, but you're not exactly a good guy."

"Because I lied to you," he said it matter-of-factly without excuse or apology.

"And you spied on my friends."

"I had a job to do."

"About that job," she asked. "What happens now? The Water Guppies are my friends, more like my grandmothers. No one wants anything bad to happen to their grandmother."

"Poppy isn't talking, but we have enough evidence to put her away. She was using her position as a loan officer at a large bank in Chicago, and her connections there, to determine which companies' stocks would be affected by mergers, loans, or inability to pay back loans. She then called her boyfriend Brad and told him how to invest their money. They even created a joint bank account for him to transfer their money into after selling off parts of their portfolio. She felt confident no one would discover the account since no one she worked with knew she had any connection to Arizona. She never discussed her personal life at work."

Meg eased into the padded chair beside his bed. She pressed her lips together tightly.

Andi's heart ached for her friend. She knew Meg's attraction to the man was waging war against her fears. On the way to the hospital, Meg said she was afraid Mack would send The Water Guppies to prison. She was also afraid of entering into another doomed relationship, assuming he was attracted to her.

Meg glanced at Andi and then spoke to Mack, "I gather you followed the money trail from their bank account to the investments."

"Exactly." A smile tugged at his lips. "We also checked Poppy's navigation system in her car. She drove to Andi's cabin the night you were hiding there. Poppy also has a huge bump on her head where Andi said she hit the intruder with a skillet."

He glanced over at Andi, and she gave him a small smile. She wanted to scream, *I was right,* but she remained silent. *I knew the intruder might be Poppy!*

"How did you end up at Euphoria Lane?" Meg asked.

Andi held her breath, wanting to make sure she heard the answer.

"We received a tip from a banker here in Arizona," Mack said. "He thought it was odd that his client, a retired woman, was incredibly lucky in the stock market and wanted us to check into it. Lorraine was the client. After we looked into her investments, we discovered a pattern and found Brad. We didn't discover he was dating Poppy until a few days ago. By the way, her real name isn't Poppy."

Meg cringed, and he laughed.

"They're not related," Mack said. "If that's what you were thinking. It was a story they concocted to cover their tracks."

"Fooled us." She shook her head. "Why did Brad pretend to be an exterminator?"

That was another question Andi had wanted to ask. Meg was doing a good job of getting information out of him.

"Posing as an exterminator was a legitimate-looking way for him to spy on The Water Guppies," Mack said. "After Poppy moved her furniture out of the condo she'd rented, I found a vial of ants under the kitchen sink. Since one and one make two, I'm going to say she planted the ants in the clubhouse to trick you into letting Brad come in and pretend to work as an exterminator. Before you ask, he stole the van and equipment inside."

"They went to a lot of trouble to execute this elaborate charade," Meg said.

"They had a lot to lose."

Meg frowned. "What happens to our neighborhood grandmas now?"

"Nothing."

His voice didn't give away any emotions, but Andi could swear she spotted a twinkle in his eyes.

"Nothing?" Meg repeated, clearly finding that hard to believe. "Are you sure?"

"Positive." He took a sip of water from the cup on his tray and made her wait for him to explain. "Poppy isn't talking, Brad isn't alive to talk, and neither is Lorraine's cousin. To top it all off, The Water Guppies made more investments than just the suspicious, highly lucrative ones."

A big smile spread across Meg's face. "You're saying it would be difficult to prove they weren't just lucky."

"Not impossible, but difficult. I also convinced my boss that the press would be bad for us once the photographer started taking pictures of Lorraine, who—"

"Looks just like Santa's wife," Meg said. "She plays it up by wearing *a lot* of red."

Andi could see the headlines. *Feds throw Mrs. Claus in jail!*

"And it's getting close to Christmas." He shrugged it off. "No one's pressing to put these grandmas behind bars—not when they have the mastermind."

"Are they blaming you for not making a case against Lorraine?" Meg asked, concern creasing her brow.

"Me? No." He smiled up at her. "They had to talk me out of retirement to do them a *favor*. They were lucky they didn't have to take another investigator off another case to spy on a bunch of senior citizens. As I said, they have the mastermind. Everyone's happy."

"I do have another question." Meg paused a moment. "Why did you tell Andi to take The Water Guppies away from the condo complex? We all knew you were a federal investigator sent here to spy on them. They could have kept on running, and then you would have gotten into trouble."

He looked sheepishly up at her. "Yes, I could have gotten into trouble *if* I hadn't already planted a tracker on your SUV."

"What?!" Meg's eyes widened in surprise.

What?! Andi's jaw dropped.

Meg narrowed her eyes. "You didn't know I would be driving!"

"I did once you drove over to Andi's. When you walked up to her door to grab the ice chest she'd left outside, I rushed over to your vehicle and attached the tracker underneath the front bumper. Then I hid in front of the neighbor's car parked in their driveway until after you drove off to pick up Lorraine and her friends."

Meg crossed her arms over her chest. "Was it all a test to see if they felt guilty enough to run away?"

"No. Not at all. I knew their lives were in danger, and I

didn't want to see a bunch of nice older ladies blown up or gunned down."

She cringed at his words. "So, you do have a heart."

"Yes, I have a heart." He ran his finger over her hand, which was resting on the side of the bed. "Meg, I hated not being able to tell you the truth. When I took this job, I never dreamed I would meet someone special, someone I want to spend more time getting to know."

Meg glanced at Andi, who nodded for her to speak her mind.

"My ex-husband lied to me—repeatedly," Meg said. "I never got over it. I don't give my trust easily."

"I understand," he said. "And if I could go back in time and turn down the assignment—I still wouldn't have."

Andi's eyes widened.

Meg blinked repeatedly and then stared at him. "What?"

"If I hadn't taken this assignment, I wouldn't have gotten to know you. I also wouldn't have been able to make sure a zealous investigator didn't try to press charges against Lorraine and her friends. All I can do right now is try to assure you that I *could not* divulge my identity and hope that my actions reveal to you my true character."

Meg glanced down at the floor and took a couple of minutes to process his words. To his credit, he sat patiently, waiting for her to speak.

Finally, Meg said, "I can see how you were in a bind. I can also see how The Water Guppies were lucky to have you on their case."

He ran his finger over her hand again. "Does that mean we can start over?"

Meg gave a slow nod. "We can—as long as you don't lie to me again."

He crossed his heart. "I promise I'll always be truthful with you—even when I know you won't like what I have to say."

She chuckled. "What now?"

"I'm hoping you'll continue to visit me while I'm stuck here, and after I'm released, I would like to take you out on a real date."

She smiled, her heart obviously melting. "I would like that."

Andi slipped out of the door, knowing her friend was in good hands.

****

The following week, Andi opened the clubhouse door while she held a bag of cooking supplies against her hip. "I hope everyone can make it tonight."

"Minus Poppy," Meg said, following her in with a box of ingredients.

"Minus Poppy." It had only been ten days since the baking lesson that had started it all, but it seemed like a year.

They sorted the supplies and ingredients onto the kitchen island and then set the oven to preheat.

The French doors suddenly swung open. "I hope you haven't started without me." Roxie sashayed inside, wearing her leopard-print jumpsuit and carrying two bottles of rum.

"I see you're prepared for the evening." Meg pulled down a glass from an overhead cabinet and placed it down on the kitchen island for the newcomer.

"Aren't you drinking with me?" Roxie appeared insulted.

"Luke is bringing Moscato with him," Andi said. "That's our drink of choice."

Roxie rolled her eyes. "I know." She placed her bottles beside the glass. "Wimps."

"Luke and Mack are picking up the garlic bread and salad," Meg added, ignoring the insult and sounding a bit giddy.

The doors swung open again, and Irene carried in two pans covered with aluminum foil. She laughed at a conversation she had started with Martha and Lorraine outside the clubhouse. They all appeared refreshed and carefree. Freedom looked good on them.

Lorraine placed her pans down on top of the stove. "The lasagna is ready to throw into the oven. By the time we finish prepping lasagna pans for each of you to take home to cook later, dinner will be ready for us to eat."

"I can almost taste it now," Martha said. "In the meantime, pour us all some rum, Roxie."

Andi removed a cylinder of plastic cups from her bag. "Anyone want a soda?"

Roxie laughed. "They don't want a kid's drink."

"Speak for yourself," Lorraine said. "I'll start with soda."

"I'll start and end with rum." Irene chuckled as she sidled up next to Roxie.

Andi noticed two familiar figures walking past the window. "One minute. I'll be right back." She rushed out through the doors and jogged a couple of yards to catch up with Emma and Nina, the two young women who were fighting over a fickle boyfriend. They wore swimsuits with beach towels tied around their waists. They were also talking and smiling at one another while they carried tote bags toward the pool.

Andi planted her hands on her hips. "Am I hallucinating?"

The girls stopped and turned. Emma looked embarrassed. "No, you're not hallucinating."

"Or dreaming," Nina said. "We made up. We're friends again."

Emma shifted her bag to the other hand. "You were right. We shouldn't have let a guy get between us. The jerk left me, too."

Nina smiled at her friend. "We made a pact never to let a man get between us again."

"Unless he's a millionaire." Emma chuckled.

"Billionaire," Nina corrected.

"I'm glad you got your priorities straight." Andi wondered how long their truce would last. Their feelings of friendship obviously didn't run deep, or they wouldn't have let that shallow guy work a wedge between them in the first place. *Or they could be too young to think about the big picture.* "I hope you keep your promise to each other." She thought about Meg, waiting for her inside. "Good friends are hard to come by."

When she rejoined the group, they were all telling jokes while Irene started browning hamburger for the meat sauce. Meg placed a rectangular baking pan in front of each of them on the kitchen island.

"While this is browning," Irene said, "we're going to prepare the noodles and the cheese filling." She placed a pan next to a pot that was large enough to boil half a dozen lobsters. The package of lasagna noodles on the counter indicated the huge pot was for those.

Andi handed ingredients over to Irene as she called them out. "Aside from cooking, what are you ladies going to do now that you don't have to hire lawyers?"

"Help plan your wedding," Lorraine said. "We promise not to get in your mother's way, but between all of us, we do have enough wedding experience to put one amazing shindig together overnight."

Roxie poured herself another cup of rum. "And I have connections to almost any venue or vendor in the valley. I can cut your costs in half."

"Would I have to get married at the racetrack?" Andi asked with a smirk.

"Funny," Roxie said. "I see you found your sense of humor now that no one is trying to kill us all."

"Speaking of killing," Martha said. "Look who's coming in the door."

They all turned to find Gladys and her daughter.

"Hello," Andi said. "What a surprise."

Gladys stepped forward. "Andi, I wanted to thank you for all you did to find the real murderer. I also want to thank whoever left the envelope under my doormat."

"Envelope?" Andi's gaze traveled from one woman to another. No one looked like they knew what she was talking about.

Gladys's daughter stepped forward, next to her mother. "Inside the envelope was five hundred dollars and a note that said to pay off her credit cards so she could stay in the condo."

Andi glanced at Lorraine.

"It wasn't me," Lorraine said.

"It wasn't me either," Martha said.

"Me either," Irene said.

Roxie walked over to a pile of paper plates, handed them to Gladys, and then gestured toward a line of folding tables they had set up earlier that day. "If you two want to stay for dinner, you can set the tables."

Gladys's eyes twinkled. "That would be nice."

Lorraine handed them each red and white checkered tablecloths. "When you're done, we'll fill you in on how to make Irene's lasagna."

Irene hummed a tune while she worked on her sauce.

Andi picked up a box of plastic forks and a pile of napkins, then joined Gladys's daughter. "Are you going to be okay with your mother staying here on Euphoria Lane?" Andi asked while folding napkins in half. "I know you wanted her to go back home to Ohio with you."

The young mother of five boys blew out a heavy breath. "After what's happened to her, I'm just glad she's not going to be living in a jail cell. I realize I was selfish, and I can't do that to her."

Gladys smiled at the two of them as she placed plates down. "How many people are we expecting?"

"With the two of you joining us," Andi said. "There will be ten."

"That many?" Gladys glanced back at The Water Guppies. "Are you sure we aren't intruding?"

"Positive," Andi said. "Since you're planning on sticking around, I think it might be a good idea for you to become a Water Guppy. They're a good group of women to have as friends."

Gladys smiled. "I could use some more friends."

The three of them finished up and then placed folding chairs around the tables. When they returned to the kitchen area, they watched Irene show everyone how to layer the lasagna, sauce, sausage, and cheese mixture. Each woman placed aluminum foil over their pan and then placed it in the refrigerator to take home with them after dinner.

"Perfect timing!" Irene opened the oven door, and the aroma of Italian cooking filled the room.

The French doors suddenly swung open again.

"Speak of perfect timing," Andi said as she watched Mack enter the clubhouse, carrying their bottle of Moscato. Luke walked in behind him, carrying a paper grocery bag. "When's dinner ready? I'm starved."

"As soon as I warm up the bread," Irene said. "I hope you remembered to bring it."

Luke placed a quick kiss on Andi's lips and then removed the loaf of bread from the bag and handed it to Irene. He glanced over at the pans she had uncovered. "Looks delicious!"

Mack handed the bottle to Meg. "Is there an opener in one of these drawers?"

She beamed up at him. "What? They didn't teach you how to search drawers in spy school?"

He chuckled. "I'm not...never mind."

Martha grinned as she took the big bag from Luke and then poured the small bags of salad mix into large bowls. "Did anyone bring dessert?"

Andi lifted her finger into the air. "I brought chocolate-covered cashews with sea salt."

Roxie's eyes twinkled with mischief. "What? No bull's eye cookies?"

Martha slapped Roxie with a tea towel. "Bite your tongue!"

Roxie practically busted a gut laughing.

Each of The Water Guppies carried items to the table and soon were all ready to sit.

"We should say a prayer," Martha said.

"You pray, while I toast," Roxie said. "Here's to staying alive."

"And to good friends," Andi added, lifting her cup.

"And new friends," Mack said, lifting his to Meg's.

Gladys lifted her cup. "And here's to a smart detective."

As if on cue, the French doors swung open, and Andi's sister, Jessie, stepped inside with her boyfriend, Derrick.

"I heard I could find you here," Jessie said.

Andi jumped up from the table. "You're back!"

Meg excused herself and walked over to greet them as well. "Perfect timing. We just sat down to eat."

Andi shared a conspiratorial smile with Meg.

"Perfect timing is right," Andi said, thanking her lucky stars her sister arrived home after she had closed the case. More proof Jessie hadn't made a mistake hiring Andi to work for her agency.

Jessie must have caught the look and furrowed her brow. "What did we miss while we were gone?"

"Nothing," everyone else in the room said, and then broke into laughter.

Andi's Chocolate Covered Cashews
Easy Crockpot Recipe

Makes 6 dozen

Ingredients

One and a half 16 oz bags of roasted cashews with sea salt
(Can substitute peanuts)
One 24 oz bag of semisweet chocolate morsels
One 10 oz bag of dark chocolate morsels
Two 12 oz bags of white baking chips (morsels)

Parchment or waxed paper

Directions

Pour the cashews into the crockpot first, then layer the
other chocolate morsels/chips on top.
Cover with lid and cook on low setting for an hour.
Stir well and then drop by spoon onto parchment or wax
paper spread over a kitchen counter or
over cookie sheets. Refrigerate until firm – approximately
one hour.

I left mine on the table to set while I went to the movies,
and they were ready when I returned.

These can be frozen.
Separate layers with parchment or waxed paper.

EXCERPT OF EUPHORIA IN THE DESERT

(Roxie and The Water Guppies star in this short story spin-off of Euphoria Lane.)

CHAPTER ONE

Grace Blackwell stepped inside the suite booked for her at the palatial Scottsdale, Arizona resort. She pulled her worn suitcase inside behind her, wondering if this weekend was too good to be true. The deal of a lifetime had provided her with a luxurious home away from home, but she had to hold up her end of the bargain she'd made with a mega movie star. If all went well, her embarrassingly low bank balance would increase by ten thousand come Monday morning.

Her eyes widened as she took in the large flat-screen television and gas fireplace situated across from the elegant, tufted sofa that looked comfortable enough to sleep on. The sliding glass door near an overstuffed side chair opened up to the golf course. *Nice!*

She scanned the kitchenette equipped with a medium-sized fridge, microwave, stovetop, and a single-serve coffee maker next to a carousel filled with a wide variety of K-Cups. She stopped to open a cabinet and found crystal wine glasses, a silver ice bucket, and a corkscrew opener. She lifted a brow in approval. Continuing her search, she found real coffee cups, not disposable ones. "So this is how the other half lives," she said to the empty room. "I could get used to this."

She pulled the strap of her camera case over her head and placed it—along with her purse—on the circular, glass dining table. Hunger pangs reminded her that she hadn't eaten anything since lunch—over nine hours ago. She found a basket filled with snacks on the granite kitchen counter and reached beyond the cookies and crackers for a bag of chips. "Brad did say everything was free."

A loud knock at the door made her jump. *Who could that be?*

She'd told the front desk not to give out her room number. She didn't want the other paparazzi she'd lured to Scottsdale to discover her secret.

The knock turned into insistent pounding.

She rushed over to the door and peered through the peephole. There was no mistaking the pink, beehive hairstyle. "Roxie?" she whispered.

"Open the door! I know you're in there," the eccentric, retired hairdresser screeched. "The security guard called me. He doesn't want—"

Grace tugged open the door on the word *security*. "Shh! Get inside! And make it fast!"

"Don't talk to your mother that way!" Roxie, wearing a leopard-print, spandex jumpsuit with gold stilettos, sashayed around Grace with triumph written all over her face. The overpowering aroma of rose perfume followed.

Before Grace could shut her door, another one in the long hall opened. A tall man, wearing a dark tailored suit, stepped out of a room near hers. He reminded her of James Bond—the Pierce Brosnan James Bond. He also looked no older than forty-five, which made him close to her in age. Butterflies took flight in her stomach.

"Hi." Grace smiled, feeling like a silly schoolgirl with a crush. She hoped the hunk hadn't heard Roxie, but she knew there was no way he could have missed *that* voice.

He eyed her suspiciously and leaned forward as if trying to glance into her room.

"Bye." She quickly stepped backward, trying to obstruct his view. She closed the door behind her, and with a quick spin on her heel, turned to face her mother. "What are you doing here?"

"One of the security guards called me," Roxie said. She began opening the cabinets in the kitchenette to inspect their contents. "He recognized you from a picture I had hanging in my beauty salon. He used to stay with his mother during her appointments. *He* knows how to tend to his mother's needs."

Grace rolled her eyes.

Roxie glanced back at her. "He also knows you're one of those paparazzi. This resort is not going to allow anyone to ruin some splashy wedding going on this weekend."

"You can tell Mr. Perfect Son that I have permission to be here."

"No, you don't! He made it perfectly clear that I'm to take you home with me." Roxie examined one of the wine glasses by flicking it with her long, fuschia-colored fingernail. The anticipated clink followed. "Hmm, real crystal." She returned the glass to its home in the cabinet. "How are you paying for this place? Did you rob a bank?" She stared directly at Grace. "Or worse?"

"No! I..." *If I don't tell her the truth, she'll cause a scene and probably drag me home by my hair like she did when I was four.* "I know where Brad Petri is really getting married—and it's not in Arizona like some people think. After his publicist's new intern admitted she'd accidentally told me the truth, Brad made me a deal."

"What kind of deal?" Roxie crossed her arms over her chest and glared.

"If I stay here at the resort, all expenses paid, and make it look like I'm secretly taking pictures of the happy couple, he'll forward me three exclusive photos of his real wedding, plus he'll pay me a bonus."

Roxie's brow furrowed. "Why would he do that? He has to know you'll sell those three photos for a lot of money."

"If I can convince everyone that the wedding is being held here in Scottsdale, this place will be flooded with reporters and paparazzi, leaving him a much better chance of tying the knot—at a different location—without being disturbed. That is worth a ton of money to both him and his filthy-rich fiancée. This is the wedding of the decade, after all. It's not every day that the biggest actor in the world marries into the biggest political family in the country."

Roxie lifted a bag of cookies out of the basket. "You think you can really convince the entire world that Brad Petri is in this resort—when he's not?"

"I already have," Grace said smugly. "Before I left California this morning, I photoshopped a picture of Brad to make it look like he was exiting his limo in front of the resort, and then I posted it online. Fast forward eleven hours—I catch two other paparazzi sneaking around the parking lot. This place will have more photographers than guests by morning."

Roxie grinned and opened the bag. "You get your smarts from me."

"Yeah," Grace said. Her mother wasn't dumb, but her father was the bright one. He taught history at a community college and left Roxie before she ruined his life. They say opposites attract, but you rarely hear that opposites stay together. "Well, it was good seeing you again. I need to unpack and then get back to work. If you want, you can grab a few more snacks from the basket before you leave. I don't want this to be a totally wasted trip for you."

Grace walked over to her suitcase and then pulled it into the bedroom.

Roxie ignored the not-so-subtle hint to leave and followed her daughter while eating her mini chocolate chip cookies. "Nice digs."

"Yes, they are," Grace said with a sigh. An inviting king-sized bed took up most of the room. Grace parked her bag next to the dark blue bed runner that created a stripe across the white down comforter. She didn't need to feel the sheets to know they were Egyptian cotton. *They have to be.* "Roxie, I don't want to be rude, but I have a job to do."

"Yeah, I wouldn't want to force you to do anything rude." Roxie ran her hand over the comforter. "Especially when the last time you visited your frail, old mother was five years ago."

Grace walked to the closet, laughing loud and hard. "You? Frail?"

"Yes, me. Besides, you said this Brad guy is paying the bills. He's loaded. Imagine the damage we could do to an unlimited expense account. Does it include the spa? And what about the resort's boutiques?" Roxie waved away her own questions. "Let's assume it does. We deserve a memorable mother-daughter weekend."

How many years has it been since I've been back to Arizona? Maybe it has been five years. Grace shook her head, forcing any feelings of guilt to backpedal away from her. *I shouldn't feel guilty. Roxie didn't let guilt get in her way when she gave custody of me to my father when I was six years old.* It would have been easier for Grace to handle her abandonment issues if she'd had Buddy, her older brother, around while she was growing up. Roxie had decided to keep him around to help her open her beauty salon.

Grace didn't have time to analyze her feelings or deal with her mother's antics right now. "I have more fake pictures I have to create and put online, then I have to run around the resort pretending to search for Brad," she said. "I don't have time for mother-daughter anything!" With irritation building, Grace tugged open the closet door with more force than she'd intended.

Roxie gasped.

"Don't pretend to be..." Before Grace could finish her remark, she glanced down into the closet and found a man sitting on the floor with a white, plastic laundry bag over his head. A cord had been cut from the resort's clothes iron and used to tie the bag tightly around the man's neck to cause suffocation.

Grace's jaw fell open, and then her legs wobbled as they started to collapse. Roxie caught her under the arms and pulled her back, away from the body, until she could sit on the bed.

"You'll be fine, you'll see. I've seen more than my share of stiffs." Roxie patted her on the shoulder and then inched forward on her stilettos, bent down, and pressed her fingers to the man's wrist to check for a pulse. "He's dead all right." She released the man's hand and then stood, her bones creaking with the effort. "On the bright side, he didn't die from poisoned snacks. We can still eat all we want."

"Mom!" Grace scolded, while the horrifying scene threatened to haunt every hour of sleep for the rest of her life. She hugged herself tightly, wishing she were anywhere else but there. Her gaze traveled down the burgundy long-sleeved shirt the man wore to a mustard stain on the left cuff near where his hand rested on his jean-clad knee. She knew that stain. She knew the outline of his body. She knew the scuff marks on his worn tennis shoes.

"Now you call me Mom—not Roxie? Who knew one dead body could erase a lifetime of resentment?"

"Would you forget that for five minutes?" Grace pointed to the closet, while her head throbbed and tears welled in her eyes. "I know this guy. We dated last year. I dropped a hot dog with mustard on his sleeve. He never tried to get the stain out."

Roxie raised her brows in apparent interest. "Your brother told me about some guy you caught cheating with your best friend. Is that him?"

Grace nodded.

"The one you threatened to kill?"

Grace nodded.

"In front of a room full of witnesses?"

Grace nodded.

Roxie stared her down. "Did you kill him?"

"Of course not!" Grace's chin quivered as she tried to hold back her hysteria. "But the police will think I did."

"No, they won't." Roxie patted her arm. "Let Mommy take care of this."

"What are you going to do?"

Roxie planted her hands on her bony hips. "What any mother would do—hide the body."

ALSO BY TINA SWAYZEE McCRIGHT

Euphoria Lane – Book One
Misfortune on Euphoria Lane – Book Two
Euphoria in the Desert – Short Spin-Off
Super Jax! The Case of the Slimy Scientist
Super Witchy! – Coming 2020
Super Vampy! – Coming 2020
A 24-Karat Gold Mystery
Walking Away With Christmas – Novella
Christmas in Garland Creek
Liquid Hypnosis
Once Upon a Weekend – Short

ABOUT THE AUTHOR

Tina Swayzee McCright is a multi-award-winning author of cozy mysteries and romantic mysteries. Every puzzle is solved by a strong woman with the help of a wacky friend and the support of a good man. When Tina isn't writing, she enjoys beach vacations with her husband, The Irish Charmer, and playing with her granddaughter. She was president of the Valley of the Sun Romance Writers, has a B.S. in Communications, and an M.A. in Curriculum and Instruction. Although she was an educator for twenty-five years, she believes her greatest accomplishment was raising an amazing daughter.

You can read more about Tina's books and join her newsletter on her website: https://www.BooksbyTina.com

Made in the USA
Columbia, SC
24 February 2020